PENDRAGON RISING

Pendragon Rising

J.A. GRAHAM

CONTENTS

I dedicate this book to my wife, for letting me chase my dreams no matter how wild, and to my children for being my inspiration and muses to write a story that all would enjoy.

Prologue: The Future King

As King Arthur led his mount over the final hillside, Camelot came into view. His heart dropped as he stared upon his once beautiful kingdom. The grounds of Camelot were now stained with blood, flames, and charred remains. Arthur and his troops had rushed home from their triumphant battle in Rome. He had received a sparrow carrying an unexpected message.

The sparrow's message read, "Mordred has captured Queen Guinevere and is attempting to seize the throne. Make haste!"

After a two-week journey back to the capital of Britain, he and his troops were exhausted. Now, staring down at the wreckage of their home, sorrow added to their exhaustion. Everything they held near and dear was below, in the flames and ash. Arthur wheeled his horse around to face his men.

"The horrors spoken in our warning are true. Mordred has become a traitor to the Round Table. We will not allow him to seize our home, our country, and families! I know we are weary, but we now battle, not for conquest or for glory. We battle for our lives and our freedom. Ride with me, once more, into battle. Let us keep what is rightfully ours! We do not fear this foe! We know him! Mordred is nothing more than a pompous child who needs to be bent over the knee!"

He lifted *Ron,* the beautiful, teal, dragonwing-tipped lance, high in the air.

"FOR CAMELOT!"

In echo, all 2,500 men cried out "FOR CAMELOT!!"

Arthur turned and began the charge. His faithful commander in arms, Sir Lancelot on his right. His mentor and most trusted advisor, Merlin on his left. The horns of the Pendragon House sounded as the army came thundering down the hill. As though Mordred had been expecting the army's arrival, soldiers armed in black armor were already filing out of the kingdom's gates in droves. They created square formations bordering the castle gates. Before the army had even reached the bottom of the hill, more than 3,000 soldiers gathered to defend the traitor. Arthur was almost in disbelief. How did Mordred have so many soldiers at his disposal? Arthur wondered what empty promises of gold, land, and power Mordred had offered these men. He scanned the scene looking for his traitorous nephew but did not see him among the ranks of soldiers. At that moment, he heard a shrill battle cry from atop the castle wall.

"Do not let them in! Hold formation! We outnumber them! We cannot lose!"

Arthur could not let his men believe that, though he knew odds were not in their favor. He led his charge faster, and extended his lance, gleaming golden and ready to attack as the enemy drew near. He closed his eyes for one moment and thought to himself, *"If this is to be my last battle, let the power of the Pendragon family flow through my veins and through my lance!"* With a quick glance over to Lancelot, they both nodded in understanding, and continued the final moments of the charge.

With the sound of a thousand clangs, the battle ensued. Arthur's army was battle-tested and was the superior force. Even though they were outnumbered, they held their own. Many soldiers in black, quickly lay lifeless on the ground as more began to join the fight. Arthur, still upon his horse, swung and stabbed *Ron* like a man possessed. He would stab one soldier, yank, flip, and slice another in one glorious sweep. He could see his noble army fighting all around him. Lancelot was wielding his double swords on foot, hacking and slicing through the enemies. Merlin stood on a small peak, calling upon blue lightning to strike ranks of soldiers. Sir Kay, another Knight of the Round Table, also on horseback, was swinging his large claymore in wide swoops. Many other Knights of the Round Table were still alive and fighting the enemy forces back toward the castle walls. The army of the Round Table seemed to be making its way through Mordred's defenses.

Just as hope flickered in Arthur's chest, fire rained from the sky.

Two figures emerged from the closing gate. One was Mordred, the traitor himself clad in silver gleaming armor. The other was a tall, slender, hooded figure. The flames were erupting from the hands of the hooded figure as they continued to walk briskly toward the battlefield.

"Uncle! Are you too tired, or just too weak, to meet me in battle?!" yelled Mordred, his voice booming, being cast across the battlefield. "Here I am, Uncle. Come face me. Let us end this ourselves!"

Arthur turned to look at Merlin, who had now taken to warding off the flames. He heard Merlin's voice in his head. *"You know what you must do. That is the only way the bloodshed will end. But know that his power is not his alone. Do not forget what we have foreseen"*

"Yes, I know, old friend. Only one of us can leave this day. The legacy of the Pendragon must be preserved" Arthur said out loud, knowing Merlin could hear him. Arthur gave Merlin a quick wink and a reassuring smile. He then turned and rode off to meet Mordred. As he rode past Lancelot, he called to him.

"I am going to face Mordred. I leave you to rescue the Queen. Tell her I love her, as I always have." Lancelot looked up to catch the eyes of his king. Lancelot began to protest, but Arthur had already ridden on.

Arthur stopped his horse as he reached Mordred. He swung his legs around and hopped from the horse in one swift movement. As his boots hit the ground, the earth trembled beneath him. He dropped to one knee and drove *Ron* into the ground with both hands. A blinding bolt of lightning split the sky, crashing down the lance's shaft. The impact forced *Ron* deep into the earth until only a few feet of the teal staff remained visible. The ground around it cracked and hardened, rippling outward as though the mountain itself bowed to the lance.

It stood anchored, immovable.

"If I fall today, let Ron remain as the symbol of my true heir," Arthur thought.

Arthur stood, and pulled his famous weapon, Excalibur, from his belt.

Mordred stared unmoved, an obsidian blade in his hand.

Calmly, Arthur spoke, "You have me, nephew. Let us see if your new strength holds up against my blade!"

He gripped Excalibur tightly with both hands. The once golden glow of the mighty sword was now glowing blood-red against the flames surrounding the two warriors.

The two lunged, blades thundering as they met. They continued to strike with little avail. Slashing, parrying, ducking, countering back and forth so ferociously that many soldiers from both sides began to encircle the two. They all wanted to watch the glorious fight that would decide their kingdom. Arthur continued to strike, his swordsmanship was apparent in every movement, but

Mordred seemed to move like a much more skilled warrior than he truly was. None of the blows landed.

"What's wrong, dear uncle? I thought you were the world's greatest knight? You can't even land a single blow! And with every strike I can see you tire!" Mordred yelled between his cackles. Mordred was right. Arthur was becoming exhausted. His muscles ached. Arthur had spotted only a single weakness in Mordred's fighting so far. In order to exploit that weakness, Arthur would have to leave himself open to a counter attack. He knew he had to take the risk, if he didn't, he would die anyway.

He had to wait for Mordred to strike. Finally, he did, wild and confident. Arthur parried Mordred's sword upward and stepped to his right. As Mordred brought his sword back down at an angle, Arthur ducked under the blow and swiped across Mordred with a backhand. The golden blade sliced through the chainmail covering Mordred's chest. Blood trickled from the gash. Outstretched, Arthur tried to stand quickly to regain his defense.

He suddenly felt a sharp pain in his ribs.

Mordred had been quick on the return strike, and the black blade was lodged between his armor and his ribs.

Both dropped to the ground. Blood began to cover the dirt as it ran from both wounds.

Arthur coughed, barely able to find breath. "Was this all worth it? Destroying the Kingdom we loved. I treated you as a son... I loved you as a son. You had everything you ever wanted. I never asked for anything in return.."

"Everything?! I didn't have everything! Gold. Women. Feasts, Yes. But I didn't have *power*. I didn't have *glory*. I didn't have *respect*." His lip curled. "You have no heir, yet you would have never named me heir. You say I am a son to you, so why would I not be? You never loved me as a *son*."

Mordred's face filled with hatred.

"And I never loved *you* as a father."

"That is what I want Uncle. Power, Glory, Respect. I want to be KING!"

Mordred sat up looking more deadly than ever, his gash beginning to slowly fade from deep red to pink, healing itself before Arthur's eyes.

"You see my new strength, Uncle? As long as I have my enchantress, I cannot be defeated. Not by you...not even by Excalibur. " His eyes gleamed at the beautiful golden sword in his dying uncle's hands. "Now I will have my power. Now, I will be the undisputed King!"

Arthur coughed again, chest burning.

"You will never wield Excalibur. For the same reason I could not give you the Kingdom. Excalibur can only be wielded by a man of pure heart. My dear Mordred, I have always sensed this darkness in you."

As the conversation with Mordred continued, Arthur felt the sword vanishing, the same as he felt his own life slipping away.

"As you see, it has already returned to the Lady. She will choose the next to find it. It is her choice alone."

Mordred looked at his own blade, mesmerized by the flames dancing on its edges and smiled. "I no longer need that cur-sed blade Uncle. I have my own."

With another bloody cough, Arthur could feel his obsidian-filled wound growing, and his strength diminishing.

"Mordred...... I AM sorry.... I did love you." Sorrow filled Arthur's ocean blue eyes as he looked up at his nephew. Arthur spoke to Merlin one last time through his mind. *"It is done. Goodbye my friend."*

With one final blood filled wheeze, white glaze spread over the king's eyes.

His body became still.

Mordred stared at his uncle's lifeless body for just a moment. Then he smiled wickedly.

"Do not be sorry, Uncle! Each story unfolds as it should. This is where your tale ends, and mine begins!

He placed his boot on Arthur's gleaming golden chest and raised his sword in the air.

"Come see your Once and Future King. His future is no more! Say your feeble goodbyes… Then kneel! Kneel before your rightful king!…*King* Mordred Lot!"

Chapter 1: The Squire

"Wake up, Arion! It is time for breakfast. Wash up and get ready. Today is your final training before you leave for Camelot," Elaine called, as she knocked gently on her son's door.

Elaine was a beautiful woman, with deep blue eyes, long sandy hair and faint smile lines across her fair skin. She returned to the kitchen of her small cottage on the outskirts of the village of South Hamtun, a small fishing village in the domain of Wessex.

Wessex, like all five of the domains of Britain, was ruled by one of King Mordred's brothers. In the case of Wessex, Sir Gawain Lot was the ruler. Sir Gareth Lot ruled Northumbria, Sir Gaheris Lot ruled Mercia, and Sir Agravaine Lot ruled East Anglia. King Mordred Lot himself ruled Logres.

The Kingdom of King Mordred had grown and now covered the entirety of Great Britain. The military was the sole focus of Mordred's rule, and they governed with an iron fist. Many of the people in the Kingdom lived in fear of the King and his Army. Those who were loyal to Arthur and the knights were either killed or quieted long ago.

Elaine and Arion had managed to live a quiet life in South Hamtun. Mordred's rule was all that Arion had ever known. Some still spoke of the days of Arthur but did so in whispers or behind closed doors.

"I'm up, I'm up..." grunted Arion, his face still in his pillow. "You seem more excited about it than I am. I'll be excited *after* my training with Sir Isaac is over."

Arion was a tall young man with a square jaw, light blue eyes, broad shoulders, and sandy brown hair. As with many young men his age, he would be finishing his role as a knight's squire, looking to become a true knight. This was one of the greatest honors in the kingdom.

Each year for the last fifteen years of King Mordred's reign, a tournament was held in Camelot. Squires would battle to prove themselves worthy of becoming knights. Squires who did not get chosen were then sent back to their villages to take on other roles such as blacksmiths, bakers, or stable attendants. You did not want to be a stable attendant.

Everyone knew King Mordred valued his soldiers above all else.

Elaine was trying to appear enthusiastic, but the thought of Arion leaving—likely forever—broke her heart. Arion was all she had, and she was all he had. Arion had never known his father and Elaine refused to speak of him.

As Arion walked into the room, she caught herself staring at him, flashes of the young boy he used to be running through her mind. He stumbled sleepily over to the table and sat down.

She smiled at him.

"Someone has to be excited," she said, trying to hide the sorrow in her voice. "You are already running late. If the knight's tournament was a competition of being on time, you'd be back home before you even reached Camelot."

Elaine gestured to the bread and jam that was sitting on the table. "Eat quickly. You need to get going."

"Yes, Mum." Arion grabbed a piece of bread, slung his armor over his head and started for the door. He stopped, kissed his mother on the head and then walked out. "I'll likely be late. If you wanted to pack my travel sack for me... I wouldn't complain!" he shouted back with a grin.

As he walked toward the fields, many villagers were already fast at work. The smell of the sea was thick in the air as it was every morning.

Men stood on the fog-covered docks collecting their nets full of fish from the night's cast. Women prepared the storefronts, setting out the many goods and wares to be sold. A few offered warm greetings, but others kept their eyes low. Mordred's soldiers patrolled the village as they did most villages. The villagers had grown accustomed to keeping to themselves beyond doing their duties or greeting customers.

The training fields of South Hamtun were on the backside of the Village Square. Lined with stables, it was a vast open field, often a place found with practicing squires and knights. Children played with balls and wooden swords, mimicking the squires' training.

Arion didn't want to admit it aloud, but excitement buzzed in his chest. He longed to prove himself in the tournament.

His mentor, Sir Isaac, was an old knight who quite frankly should have laid down his shield many years ago. Isaac's training style was more "watching and criticizing" than "teach and spar". Arion often saw other knights sparring with their squires during training, unlike Sir Isaac. It hardly seemed that Arion needed the sparring though. Arion was a gifted talent with any weapon he touched. Sir Isaac often joked that he must have been born with a sword in his hand. Weapons always felt strangely natural in his hands. Even the ones he disliked.

As Arion approached his stable, there was a rack of weapons waiting for him. Sir Isaac was not yet to be found. He often left during training to get a warm drink or lunch, only to return to criticize Arion, as though he had been there the whole time.

Arion looked at the rack.

Knights of the kingdom trained dreaming of joining a specific order of knights. Some trained for range, others for horseback, and others for close combat. Arion felt most comfortable with the cold hard steel of a sword in his hands, but the tournament assigned weapons at random, in the close combat trials he would be competing in.

He could hear Sir Isaac's words in his head. *"In order to win the tournament, you must be the complete warrior. No weapon should feel like a weakness."*

He sighed and grabbed a short, clubbed mace, the weapon he disliked most.

After what seemed like hours of attacking sparring dummies, Arion's muscles ached. Straw from the dummies littered the ground.

He finally stopped to rest and sat down to drink from his water bladder and wipe sweat from his face.

As he stood, ready to begin again, he noticed a rider approaching. An old man in worn armor atop a gray steed.

Arion straightened himself, then bowed.

"Sir Isaac."

"Morning, Arion," Isaac slid off his horse with a pained grunt. "You need more time with the lance. It is your weakest weapon. And make sure that when striking with that mace, you pivot off the back foot to maintain balance." He offered a crooked smile.

Arion gave a sideways glance at Isaac. "Yes, sir. I didn't realize you were watching."

Isaac smiled again, this time showing off his yellowed teeth. "You think just because I am an old man, I am blind? I was back some ways, but my eyes were upon you."

"Of course, sir. I was just...focused."

Isaac snorted. "Focused, were you? Then I assume that you also did not notice the man that I have brought with me," Isaac gestured to the other side of the horse.

A man stepped forward, draped in orange robes, steel gray eyes and nearly white-blonde hair, cut short. His eyes seemed to carry much pain and sorrow, making him look much older than he likely was. The man extended a hand.

"Hello young lad. Your good knight was just showing me around the village. I assume you're entering the knight's tournament in Camelot?"

"Yes, sir," replied Arion. Something about the man's eyes unsettled him. "Sir Isaac believes I have a chance at winning... May I ask your name?"

The man smiled politely.

"I am simply an old traveling monk. I offer my services to those who need it, should they need a prayer or blessing. I am also headed to Camelot. I will be assisting in the health ward at the tournament."

"Then I look forward to seeing you there. Please excuse me... I need to continue my training. It would seem, I need to spend more time with the lance." He shot Isaac a look. "I bid you a good day." Arion bowed.

"Good day, lad," the monk chuckled. "Good Isaac, I must return to my ward. I shall see you both at the Tournament."

He began to walk away, then paused. He turned and watched Arion for a moment. Arion caught the monk's gaze; the monk winked and politely smiled, before continuing down the path.

Isaac clapped his hands.

"Enough standing around. Choose your lance, and let us begin our work."

For the first time in a long time, Sir Isaac, unsheathed his chipped, battered old sword.

"This is your final lesson. Your goal is to beat me with that lance. I'll use my best weapon, while you use your worst. We'll use blunted weapons, but the last to yield is the victor. Begin when ready."

Arion grabbed the blunted lance and turned to face his master. Both men bowed and took a defensive stance.

Isaac, with shocking speed, made a sweep at Arion's legs. He swiped from the right to left. Arion blocked the attack with the shaft of the lance, and countered with a jab to Isaac's shoulder. Isaac barely flinched, bringing his sword slicing upward, catching Arion in the hip. He hissed in pain and quickly moved backward out of reach of Isaac's sword.

Arion kept Isaac at bay with the lance's reach. Arion jabbed left, then right. Isaac again showed alarming quickness for an old man and dodged both attacks cleanly. Arion stabbed low, and Isaac moved his leg to dodge. Arion then snapped the lance tip up hard to Isaac's inside thigh.

The old knight faltered.

Arion spun, slammed the shaft against Isaac's back, then swept his knee, dropping him to the ground. Flipping his lance in his hands, he placed the tip to the throat of his master.

Isaac raised his hands, breathing heavily.

"I yield, I yield!" he laughed. "I may be as glad as you are that today your training ends. I am getting too old for this. Well done, lad. Very well done."

The old knight stood up, wiping the sweat from his brow.

"Arion, I believe you are as prepared as ever. And I must say...you truly do have a gift." He said, voice thick with pride. "I have trained knights for many moons. You may be the most complete squire I have ever trained. I have no doubt you will reach the ranks of the Sabaton Knights—one of the elite."

"Come now, prepare your things. We leave for Camelot tomorrow, first crow of the rooster."

Arion beamed. "Thank you, Sir. It has been a pleasure learning from you. I will make you proud, this I swear."

They clasped wrists. Sir Isaac looked at his squire.

"Two days from now... I hope to call you brother... and no longer my squire."

Chapter 2: The Castle

Morning came as though the night had simply not existed. Arion had been awake before the rooster stirred. The excitement and butterflies had run heavy in his stomach since waking. Arion made for the kitchen, but froze when he heard his mother's voice.

"Arion! The sun is rising. You need to be waking! Breakfast is ready!" she called, startling him.

"I'm already awake," he said, stepping into the kitchen. "I thought I was the only one. Any sign of Sir Isaac?"

If he arrived late to the tournament, he would be disqualified. They were expected to be checked in before the sun reached its peak in the day sky. He went to the table, and began shoveling food into his mouth.

"Not yet," Elaine said, watching him devour breakfast. "But slow down or you'll choke. What a shame it would be if you were defeated by your breakfast before you ever got to show your skill with a weapon."

Her laugh faded, replaced by a seriousness Arion couldn't ignore. Tears welled in her eyes.

"I want you to know I believe in you," she said, barely a whisper. "No matter what happens, I am, and always have been, proud of you. You are the best thing that ever happened to me. If you do get chosen as a knight… please do your best to return home when you can."

Arion looked up as he shoved the last piece of bread in his mouth, and managed a smile. "You know I will. I love you, Mum. I will honor you. I'll honor our name, just like my father did."

Arion said this carefully, hoping his mother would finally tell him more about his father.

Elaine's gaze softened for a moment, then quickly hardened.

"Your father was a valiant knight, the most courageous and kindest of them. A great swordsman… but even that wasn't enough to keep him alive in the Kings' War. He died fighting for King Arthur. You know this."

This was the only thing she had ever told him about his father. The single thread of his heritage. Arion leaned forward.

"Mum, I just wish I knew more about him. I just want to know where I come from."

"I know," she whispered, holding back tears. "You know I cannot. Not now, anyway." She drew a shaky breath. "Sir Isaac is here. You must go."

The timing felt too convenient, and Elaine's relief at the interruption was impossible to miss.

"I love you, my son," she said quickly, kissing his forehead with a trembling hand. "May the Gods watch over you."

"I love you too," Arion replied. He grabbed his travel sack and armor and wrapped her in one last embrace. She held him longer than he expected. Elaine knew that she would not be seeing her son again anytime soon. Arion turned toward the door. She grabbed his wrist.

"Wait. I want you to have this. It was your father's." She unclasped a necklace from her neck. Arion had always known her to wear the necklace, but never knew where it came from. On the chain was a circle pendant with the Roman numeral I in the center. Behind the number were two crossed swords. "This is the only thing I have left of him. He would want you to have it. It has kept us safe all these years. Hopefully it can continue to protect you."

She put the chain around his neck. Arion looked down at the pendant. It must have been one of the pendants given to Arthur's warriors. Trying to hold back tears, they both hugged again. Arion wiped his eyes and turned to the door. As he stepped outside, she ran to the doorway.

"Stay safe, Arion! I love you!"

Arion waved back to his mother, excitement filling him once again. That excitement was quickly squelched by Sir Isaac. "Well, we have about four hours until we reach Camelot. Make yourself comfortable."

The first hour went by quietly. As they crested over a small hill they solemnly passed by a village that was still smoldering from fresh flames. A flag bearing Mordred's banner was sticking threateningly from the center of the carnage. People's shops, clothes, and homes were reduced to ash. Arion couldn't help but feel for the villagers who survived the massacre.

Isaac caught Arion's gaze and broke the silence. "It wasn't always this way. But things change."

He gave Arion a comforting smile. "I was just a young lad the first time I traveled to Camelot. The world was much different then."

Arion looked at Sir Isaac. "Different how?"

"Well, gold and red banners of King Arthur were hung from every village. Markets were packed full of people; music played in the streets. Knights were more than just enforcers in those days. They cared for the people. Their compassion, their honor, is what made me want to become one myself. Arthur promoted those qualities. He led men to become better men."

"Did you ever meet King Arthur?" Arion asked.

"Once, after my trials. The trials back then were not like today. They were less about skill and strength and more about courage and resilience. But just as you will meet King Mordred if you pass your trials, I met Arthur. He knighted me, and I swore my oath to him. He was a great man and I was proud to serve him."

Arion thought about the world now. How it seemed less...hopeful.

"I wish I could have seen Britain back then. Do you wish you could go back?"

"Britain is still Britain," Sir Isaac said simply. "The heart of our kingdom is still with the people. Kings will come and go, it is the people that must endure."

They both became silent again. Arion thought again of a world with people praising Arthur's name. People dancing freely in the streets with no fear. A world of hope. He had never seen Camelot as Isaac had. But now he longed to.

The next couple of hours they continued in silence just watching the fields blur into rolling hills until, finally, Camelot rose in the distance—grand, gleaming, and impossibly vast. Travelers poured in from every direction until their cart was swallowed by the flow.

"This is where King Arthur and the Knights of the Round Table once met," he thought, heart pounding.

Camelot unfolded before him, greater even, than the legends. Along the clear blue skyline was a massive castle wall made of marble. Each high turret and peaked roof gleamed with gold in the high sun. In the distance was the main castle. It stood highest among all the rooftops and buildings inside the walls. Pillars of marble held up the golden roof around the entire main castle and in the very center was a large balcony, which hung a giant banner.

The blood red banner waved in the wind. In the center of the banner was a red eye surrounded by a white eight-pointed star. The banner of King Mordred Lot. Dozens more were draped off the castle walls and high towers like watchful eyes.

As they drew close to the castle gates, Arion noticed three knights in pitch black armor guarding something roped off on the grounds. People were crowded around it staring and pointing. All Arion could see was a teal pole jutting out of the ground.

"Camelot, in all its glory." Isaac muttered, taking in the view.

As they pushed through the masses of people, Arion couldn't help but feel overwhelmed. They entered the huge oak gates and were surrounded by shops. There were blacksmiths, flower shops, bread makers, butchers, and farmers, all selling their wares. Hundreds of them lined the main street. There were people everywhere, buying, selling, and just strolling about. Arion had never seen so many people in one place. It was grand.

"Imagine protecting a place like this," he breathed.

He continued to look around and drink it all in. As they continued down the path, the masses of people lessened.

Arion noticed that all that seemed to remain were pairs that mimicked the dynamic between him and Sir Isaac. Squires riding and walking alongside their mentors, here for the trials.

As they passed one squire and his knight, Arion and the other squire, a lean young man with long black hair tied loosely behind his back, met eyes for a moment. They both nodded. A simple gesture between warriors.

"You ready for today?" Sir Isaac said, trying to bring Arion back to level ground. "I know there is grandeur here but do not forget why we came. I want you to see something."

Sir Isaac gave him a brief, knowing look, then turned the cart down a narrower side road.

"Sir Isaac... isn't the arena that way?" Arion asked, confused.

Isaac didn't answer. He flicked the reins and kept going.

"Arion, my boy, do not get caught up in the deceit that is paraded in front of us," Isaac said, nodding ahead, directing Arion's attention. "This is the truth of King Mordred's rule."

The farther they went, the more the illusion of Camelot's grandeur crumbled.

Lining the street, hidden behind shade, were hundreds upon hundreds of people. Their clothes were tattered; many looked feeble, and they were all staring at the passing cart. Their eyes sunken with fear as they rolled by. Some watched from alleyways; others huddled beneath broken stalls or blankets too tattered to ward off any cold.

No one spoke above a whisper.

Arion's stomach tightened.

"In Arthur's day, these people were happy, healthy and many had homes here in Camelot. These streets shone with life. Now? Mordred has allowed the rich to get richer and the poor to starve. Anyone who did not immediately kneel to his regime were either killed or cast from their homes and stripped of everything. This is but one of many streets here in Camelot. It is like this in every corner of the kingdom. In South Hamtun and all of Wessex, we are blessed to have Sir Gawain as our Lord, as he still believes in some of the old ways. He was one of the Knights of the Round Table and one of King Arthur's most trusted. But he is also a brother to the King and is just as loyal to his family as he was the Round Table. The other brothers are much more ruthless and enjoy Mordred's quick hand."

Arion swallowed hard. His earlier excitement turned to guilt. He wondered how the world could be so dark.

"And speaking of his rule," Isaac continued. "You will meet the Brothers of Lot today should you win. Be careful what you say and how you say it. While Sir Gawain may be kinder than the others, he is still a Lord under his brother's rule. You cannot trust any of the Brothers of Lot."

He flicked the reins again. "We'd best head to the tournament check-in. It's nearly time."

Many more sets of terrified eyes caught Arion's gaze as they strolled back out into the main courtyard, where the arena was erected. He was surprised they were here, near the splendor of the central courtyard.

A guard shoved a man in tattered clothes away from the entrance to the main streets. Arion's anger grew as he watched the abuse continue, and locals remained unfazed by the mistreatment. He sat in silence with the new revelation as they made their way through the final moments of their journey.

At last, they reached the large tent where the squires were checking in. Arion hopped off the cart, grabbed his leather armor and bag and turned to Isaac.

"Well," he said with a nervous laugh, "looks like this is it. Too late to back out now?"

Isaac clasped his wrist. "No fear. All honor."

With a nod, Isaac took off to find a place to store the cart and feed the horses.

Arion was left standing with his bag and armor.

With one final look around and a deep sigh, he entered the tent.

Chapter 3: The Tournament

Arion entered the tent and saw at least thirty other young men and women preparing their leathers and mail. The squire he saw earlier in the square locked eyes with him from across the tent. Again they nodded. Another squire, a young lady, politely waved as he walked by. He continued through the tent, looking for Sir Isaac's banner of green, with a grey stripe behind an emblazoned shield. This would be where his gear would be stored, along with his water bladder and any minor medical supplies. He found his bench and began lacing up his armor, as a knight entered the tent, ready to explain the rules of the tournament.

"'Ello young'uns!" the knight barked, his voice loud and boisterous behind his accent. "Me name's Morholt. I'm a Sabaton Knight and your tournament guide. So gather round! Gather round! There'll be three tests for you to choose from."

The room quieted.

"The first is a simple archery contest. Top ten archers'll get a chance to see if they can outshoot one of Camelot's aces. If you can match or best his shots, you'll take your place as a Ranger Knight."

"Next will be the joustin' contest, where you'll be tryin' to dismount each other from your horses. Being knocked off means you're out. The top ten'll again challenge one of our Charger Knights. Best him or remain saddled after a single lance, you'll take your place among 'em."

"Lastly," Morholt paused with theatrical menace. "will be the melee contest. The last four standing at the end of two rounds'll take on one of the kingdom's elite, a Sabaton Knight. If you can last in the arena without being bludgeoned, beaten, or knocked unconscious, you'll stand beside us. Obviously, this means we'll be taking a much smaller group of Sabaton Knights."

He tapped his breastplate proudly as he looked at their eager faces.

"All weapons will be blunted. Killing is an automatic disqualification. Your opponent must yield or be knocked unconscious. There you have it. Are there any questions?"

Arion swallowed. The Ranger Knights were the defenders of the castle walls and were the scouts in war. They were the elite with ranged weapons. The Charger Knights were the cavalry specialists. They were deadly on horses and led troops into battle. And the Sabaton Knights were the special forces of knights. They were trained to be great with any weapon and would typically be either tasked with protecting the King and other royals as their Guard, or as an Elite Strike Unit.

One squire raised his hand. "Is it true that each knight chosen gets a turn to try to pull out the Lance in the Stone?"

Morholt barked a laugh. "Aye, lad. Everyone's always concerned with that bloody stick. But yes. Every new knight gets a try. Many have tried. All have failed. Anything else?"

Another squire, a stout, brown haired young man called out, "How will we know when it is our turn?"

Morholt pointed toward a large wooden board shaped like a shield. "Your master-in-arms banner'll be placed on the wall behind me. We will call out your name twice. If you do not show, you will be counted as unable to perform and be removed from the competition. Are there any other questions? Nay? Then finish preparin'. We'll begin shortly. Listen for the trumpets. And remember, our Lords and King will be here to witness the Tournament. Give your best and put on a good show. Good luck young squires!"

Morholt wheeled around and left the tent.

The Lance in the Stone... that's what was roped off on the castle grounds as they were coming in. Arion had thought it was only a legend. Now that he knew it was real, winning mattered even more.

With the help of a couple younger boys, likely future squires, eager to assist, Arion finished putting on his leather and chainmail vest. Arion opted not to wear his helm as he felt being lighter would work in his favor.

By the time he had finished, there were two gamesmen setting the board. It seemed the contests would go in the order that Morholt explained them. Archery first; jousting second, and the melee last. The archery contest board was set and about to begin.

Arion knew this meant he had time.

He slipped out of the tent and crossed the courtyard in the direction of the shops. He could hear the trumpets sounding in the area of the arena signaling the start of the tournament. As he walked, something caught his eye. Rows of statues lined the courtyard that he had not noticed earlier. They were a brilliant-white marble, each carved in the likeness of a knight.

He moved along the line of busts, reading each engraved name:

Priamus, Lamorak, and Segwarides.

They were Knights of the Round Table. All had fallen or gone missing in the Kings' War.

Each had a statue with their name and a brief biography of their role and their death. Arion ran his hand across their names as he continued down the line of marble warriors.

In the center stood two larger statues.

One was a long-haired warrior that held two short swords, little armor, but fierceness in his eyes.

Lancelot.

Arion read the inscription:

"The closest companion of King Arthur Pendragon and Commander in Arms of the Round Table. Succeeded in freeing Guinevere from Camelot during the Kings' War but was not seen fleeing the castle grounds himself. Presumed dead."

Arion stared at this statue for a moment. A feeling of familiarity washed over him; something about his face, his eyes.

He shook his head. This was one of the most famous Knights to have ever lived; of course he's familiar.

He continued to the largest statue.

At once he knew who it was. No name needed to be read;

King Arthur.

He traced the carved letters:

"Known as the Once and Future King. King Arthur Pendragon was ruler of Britain and head of the Round Table."

A larger set of text read:

"King Arthur died at the hands of Mordred Lot."

Arion realized this was just as much a boast from Mordred as it was a memorial to Arthur. Mordred wanted the kingdom to be reminded who had conquered greatness.

He stood there, lost in thought, imagining so many fighting for this man. His father, dying for him.

"You feel it too, don't you?" Sir Isaac whispered as he walked up beside him. "Even his statue makes you want to kneel?"

Arion turned, surprised. "Sir Isaac! I didn't see you."

"Just arrived." Isaac's eyes stayed on Arthur's marble face. "I hope your mind is still on the task at hand. You will be starting soon."

"Already?" Arion blinked. "I didn't realize I had been out here so long. I am ready, sir."

He hesitated, glancing again at the statue of Arthur.

"Sir... I have a question."

Isaac raised a brow. "Go on, lad."

"What can you tell me of my father?"

Sir Isaac returned his gaze to the statue, and sighed.

"To tell the truth, my boy... I know very little. Your mother brought you to me when you were just a young lad. All she told me was that you had the blood of a great warrior and that she'd be honored if I took you as my squire." Isaac chuckled, reminiscing of those days. "I was too old for war by then. I decided it was likely time that I take on a squire. So I agreed." He sighed again. "That's all she told me. And that's all I know. I'm sorry."

He looked at Arion and gave him a weak smile.

Arion nodded, disappointed, but he didn't press.

"We must get back," Isaac said, placing a hand on Arion's shoulder. "Your contest will be beginning soon."

"Yes sir." Arion cast one final look at the statues.

The two turned, and walked back to the tent together.

By the time they returned to the tent, the Ranger Knight trial had concluded. The shield-shaped board now displayed the banners of the winners from the archery contest. The squires from the archery competition were finishing up packing their things and beginning to leave the tent, to take their place among the crowd.

One archer stopped and turned to Arion. It was the girl who had waved at him earlier when he first entered the tent.

"You're from South Hamtun, correct? I'm Shyla."

Before Arion could respond, she barreled on, cheerful and breathless.

"My father was born in South Hamtun. He moved north to Bristow when he met my mother. That's where I'm from. He always talked of the fishing piers, the ships docking, and the visiting travelers..." She smiled brightly. "I always dreamed of seeing it one day. Maybe you could be the one to show me around. Anyway... good luck."

She held out her hand.

"Er... thanks," Arion managed. He looked her over as he shook her hand. She looked simple, yet naturally beautiful, even in leather armor. Her strawberry blonde hair was held up tight in a bun, which showed her pale, soft skin and gleaming hazel eyes eloquently.

"I'm Arion. Congrats on winning the archery contest. Hopefully I'll be joining you shortly."

On cue, Morholt appeared through the tent flap.

"Squires entering the Charger Knight trials... on your ready!"

Shyla smirked at Arion. "Welp, I'm off to watch the rest of the tournament. Hopefully we can talk more when we get Knighted together." She winked at him. "Don't disappoint me."

She turned and disappeared out of the tent.

Arion blinked, stunned. He returned to his bench and began rechecking his armor as he listened to the joust. Nerves began to come over him.

The crowd cheered. "Girardus has fallen! We have a winner!"

The first leg of the joust was already over. He looked around at the other fifteen squires who he would be competing against in the melee tournament. He recognized the one from the square immediately. He walked up to him as he was pulling his leather cuirass over his head.

"I'm Arion. Pleased to meet you. Looks like we will be in the melee tournament together." Arion reached out his hand to say hello.

"I'm Tybout of Edinburgh," he replied. "Yes, it seems we will." He grasped Arion's wrist. "I wish the joust would hurry though. No matter the amount of training, the wait is the worst part."

Arion smiled. "Agreed. I was ready to go until we had to just sit here. Now I'm getting a little nervous."

"Glad I'm not the only one."

Arion gave him one final nod. "Well good luck out there. If we are paired, I'll give you my best. If not, I look forward to seeing you in the second round."

Tybout shook his head in agreement. "Same to you. Good luck."

Arion returned to his section and sat. He closed his eyes and listened to the crowd roar again after the sound of hooves had faded. Another joust won.

He sat in silence, tightening straps on his armor, fidgeting with his gloves as he waited for the joust to finish and time to pass. As his nerves increased, the minutes slowed. Each further minute began to feel like an hour.

Arion leaned forward, elbows on his knees, staring at the dirt floor as though it could anchor him. *Focus. You trained for this. Just breathe.*

He again tightened straps on his armor. Everything was already perfectly in place but it gave his hand something to focus on. Each tug one moment closer to his challenge.

Another cheer erupted. Another thud.

His stomach flipped. It had to be almost time.

Arion closed his eyes briefly, trying to imagine the arena the way he'd seen it from outside: square and full of the crowd surrounding it. But the image twisted—he saw the weapons rack instead, the weapons he *might* draw, the faces he *might* face. He opened his eyes and looked at those faces.

Another cheer. A trumpet sounded. And then… silence.

Moments later, Morholt returned.

"Alright lads and ladies. The time has come. Follow me."

Arion tightened the straps on his armor one last time, grabbed hold of the pendant his mother gave him, and thought of her. He stood and followed the others out of the tent.

The melee was about to begin.

Chapter 4: The Melee

Arion and the other fifteen contestants were being led to a small row of seats where they would wait for their first round match. As they made their way to the arena, Arion caught sight of the monk whom he had met in South Hamtun the previous day. The monk spotted him as well and smiled, waving to Arion.

"Good luck today!" he called. "I have decided to watch this particular contest. It is my personal favorite. Do put on a good show!"

Arion waved back. "I'll do my best! I'm just ready to start."

The monk's eyes paused for a moment on the pendant hanging from his neck. He quickly looked back up and smiled again. "I'm sure you are. Believe in yourself and you'll do great. I'm sure Sir Isaac has prepared you well."

"Yes, sir. I will," Arion said, then sat on the benches with the other squires. The arena buzzed with excitement, the crowd shifting like a living mass. Arion adjusted the straps on his gauntlets as a sudden ripple of silence swept across the stands.

King Mordred had arrived. A figure of stark power; silver armor that shone like a frozen star, crowned by a regal crimson cloak that whispered of dominion. Upon his head was a vibrant, jewel encrusted crown.

He took his seat at the highest point of the arena, where a box sat raised, draped in black and crimson banners. Flanking him on both sides sat four imposing figures, each bearing a different crest.

The boar.

The stag.

The wolf.

The fox.

The Brothers of Lot.

Agravain sat closest to Mordred, broad-shouldered and stone-faced, wrapped in a heavy black cloak. His armor was dark steel, battered and scarred, memories of his years of battles. Beside him rested Gawain, handsome and unreadable, dressed in a silver fur cloak. His smile was thin, sly, looking over the squires. On the other side was Gaheris, tall and intense, sitting perfectly still.

And finally, Gareth. Huge and hulking, he leaned forward, elbows on his knees, jaw clenched so tightly the muscles in his temple flickered. His near white armor, blinding in the sunlight.

Mordred sat between them, hand folded, observing the arena with a cold and calculated interest.

The weight of their presence pressed over the arena like a stormcloud, but Arion felt something different stir inside him. Instead, the nerves that had bothered him all morning suddenly seemed to fade. A steady calm settled in, as though he'd stepped exactly where he was meant to be.

He sat and watched the first match closely, studying the fighters' footwork and the rhythm of their strikes. The second match went much the same way.

Then, Tybout was up. Arion was excited to see his fight. He could tell by his calmness that he was a good warrior but just in case he had a chance to meet him in the next round, he wanted to study everything he could. A wide-shouldered, dark-haired squire got up and walked to the arena. Tybout's challenger.

"You got this," Arion called to Tybout as he walked into the arena. Tybout gave him a quick thumbs up in return.

He went to his corner where the tournament official brought him his weapon. A Spear. The dark haired challenger was given a spiked flail. Tybout would have to find a way to avoid the spiked ball on the end of the long chain if he wanted to be able to attack. Arion watched as Tybout took a deep breath.

The horn sounded.

Immediately the challenger swung the flail overhead and launched it toward Tybout.

He moves so quickly, Arion thought, as Tybout effortlessly dodged the attack. The flail smashed into the ground, throwing sand everywhere. Tybout stepped in to attack but the challenger pulled the flail back toward him, catching Tybout in the back. He was knocked hard into the dirt.

The crowd gasped.

"Get up," Arion thought.

The challenger launched the flail again. Tybout rolled quickly out of the way. He jumped to his feet, looking ready to keep fighting.

That's it.

The flail was thrown again. Again, Tybout sidestepped it easily. Without warning, Tybout hurled his spear.

It landed, the tip splitting the chain of the flail. The challenger yanked, but the spear made the flail immovable.

Tybout ran, jumped, and grabbed the shaft of the spear, vaulting himself toward the challenger. He landed a flying kick squarely into the challenger's chest, knocking him to the ground. Tybout pulled the spear from the ground, flipped it around, and held it to the gasping warrior's throat.

The crowd erupted in cheers. Tybout had won his match.

"He's fast and calculated. He could be a problem. I hope I don't have him in the next round." Arion whispered to himself.

Tybout bowed to the crowd and made his way back to the benches, next to Arion.

"Great match," Arion said as he clasped Tybout's wrist.

"Thanks. My back is still aching. I didn't want to chance getting hit again so I figured I would end it quickly." He said smiling. "Don't get too comfortable. You'll be up soon"

Arion looked to the crowd and saw King Mordred and his Brothers clapping in approval of Tybout's match. He continued to look around the arena and caught Shyla waving and smiling in his direction. He again went red, but returned the wave, looking away quickly.

The next match began the same as the rest, with a horn sounding—this time between two squires both wielding broadswords and shields.

The two squires were evenly matched. Their blades flashing, shields ringing as the crowd roared with every clash. For several minutes the fight surged back and forth, neither gaining ground. Gasps rippled through the stands each time steel struck a little too close.

Then, suddenly, the cheering died. A horrified hush swept across the arena. One of the squires drove his sword straight through the other's chest, the blunted tip denting the breastplate with a sickening crunch. This was no accident. It was a full, deliberate thrust.

The wounded boy collapsed, armor scraping hard against the dirt. Monks sprinted from the sideline to reach him, shouting for space. Arion saw the rise and fall of the boy's chest, barely, but he was alive.

His opponent didn't even look back. He raised both arms in tri-umph, basking in the cheers of a handful of supporters who didn't seem to care how the victory was earned. King Mordred was on his feet clapping; with the King applauding, none of the officials dared call it a disqualification.

This was supposed to be a trial, not a fight for life.

A cold realization settled into Arion's stomach:

Not every squire here had been taught honor.

Not every knight's code matched Isaac's.

And in that moment, the arena felt far more dangerous than steel alone.

By the time the shock had worn off, the next match had fin-ished. Arion tugged the strap of his chainmail one last link tighter. He was up next.

"Arion of South Hamtun! And Beldin of Gippeswyk! Take your corner!" called one of the gamesmen.

Arion rose, heart steady, and walked out into the bright square of the arena. He was shown to his corner and awaited his weapon assignment. Sir Isaac was there waiting for him.

Beldin was given a Lochaber axe, a long-shafted axe of nearly six feet. It was slim, long, and equipped with a curved blade that was hooked on the end. Arion, to his displeasure, was given a sim-ple quarterstaff equipped with a couple of iron rings on each end to increase its durability. Not ideal.

"Remember what I've taught you. It's not the weapon that makes the warrior, it's the man," whispered Sir Isaac in his ear. He clasped his shoulder. "You cannot lose if you fight with honor." Ar-ion nodded, focused.

Both squires stood and bowed. Arion looked around the square and saw many faces staring at him in the stands. He caught Shyla's eye once again. She smiled. Arion could feel his face turning red, his pulse spiking. He inhaled slowly and tried to refocus on Beldin.

He looked Beldin over, waiting for the horn to sound. Beldin wore an iron vest and chainmail sleeves. He had a leather skirt around his legs. Like Arion, he did not have any headgear.

Arion gripped his staff and shifted into a defensive stance.

The horn sounded.

The axe's dulled edge was still dangerous, but only if Beldin could deliver a clean blow. Arion planned to stay just outside of its reach. For Beldin to land a blow, he would have to swipe with the axe. If Arion could slip inside the shaft's length, he could strike Beldin's legs, which were free of any armor.

Beldin quickly attacked. He sliced twice with the axe. The second arcing slice narrowly glanced Arion's shoulder, but the hook caught his steel pauldron and jerked him forward.

Perfect.

He was pulled in close, right where he wanted to be. Beldin shook the axe to free it of the pauldron. Arion took advantage of the confusion. He flipped his staff in his hands and cracked it hard across Beldin's left shin. Before Beldin could react – finally freeing his axe—Arion reversed his grip and swept Beldin's leg out from under him. Beldin crashed to the ground.

Arion struck Beldin's armor-covered chest with the staff. It didn't do much damage, but it was so loud, the clang echoed off the courtyard. The clang disoriented Beldin, ringing in his ears. Arion lashed both of Beldin's hands with his quarterstaff.

Beldin opened his hands in pain and the axe clattered to the ground.

Arion snatched it up and placed the dull edge to Beldin's throat.

As quickly as the match started, it was finished.

"I yield!" Beldin wheezed.

The crowd erupted as Arion helped Beldin to his feet.

"You are definitely a skilled warrior," Beldin said, shaking Arion's hand. "I fear for those who face you with a much more deadly weapon."

"Thank you," replied Arion, grinning.

They bowed once more, and Beldin joined the row of defeated squires. Sir Isaac cheered loudly. "Well done, my squire. Well done!"

Arion returned to the benches with the others.

"Mate, that was a great show of skill. I knew you would be good, but that was next-level." Tybout clasped Arion on the shoulder as he sat down next to him.

"Thanks." Arion smiled, trying to hold back his elation.

The rest of the round blurred by. By the time Arion's adrenaline had worn off, they were calling for the squires to return back to the tent.

The first round was over.

Chapter 5: The Eight

Morholt returned to the tent once again. "Those that lost, 'tis time to gather yer things and either join those in the stands or return home. Many of you fought valiantly, but sadly, your road to becoming a knight ends here."

"To my winners, you'll have a short break while our officials set the matches for the next round. Use this time to receive aid, repair any armor, or rest before we begin. I'll return to get you when the time is near." And with that he exited the tent.

Arion looked around and saw the losers of the first round grabbing their equipment and clearing off their benches, some looking worse for wear. Once they exited, the tent felt empty. There were now only eight squires left. Monks were checking on each of them, asking if they needed assistance.

Arion spotted the monk that visited him, and he came briskly over.

"Great match in the first round. You fought well," the man said, looking at him proudly. "You didn't take any direct hits but I must ask, are you in any need of aid?"

His eyes fell again on the pendant, but quickly looked back at Arion.

Arion shook his head. "No. Honestly, I'm alright."

"Great. Well I'm excited to watch the next round. You are all very skilled. You can't take anyone lightly this round. One mistake could be your last." He grinned at Arion. "Well I would love to talk further but it looks like one of the other squires could use my help."

He was being waved down by a fighter with a long bleeding cut. "Good luck next round!"

Waving, Arion got up to find Tybout. Tybout was sitting at his bench, relacing his gauntlets quietly. The tent felt more tense, more hollow, now that just eight fighters remained.

Tybout glanced as Arion neared, and gave him a knowing grin. "Looks like we made the cut."

Arion laughed lightly. "Looks that way. It only gets harder from here."

"I would be worried if it didn't."

Arion sat down next to Tybout chuckling. They both sat in silence for a moment, scanning the room. Arion watched as the brutal fighter mimicked his earlier fight. Smiling widely as he thrust his imaginary sword again.

Tybout's eyes followed. The two exchanged a concerned look.

They both turned their attention to a massive, blonde fighter who was pacing like a caged bull, beating his chest and huffing with each beat.

"He'll come out swinging the first chance he gets," said Tybout quietly.

"If he can even wait that long," chuckled Arion.

They weren't mocking him, but had seen him fight already. He had won by ramming the hilt of a spear into his foe's face with terrifying force. He was incredibly strong. But incredibly predictable.

As they inspected the remaining fighters, a monk passed by, offering aid one final time. They politely declined.

They sat in silence for a moment more. The nerves began to build as the time for the next round came nearer.

Finally, Tybout stood, rolling his shoulders out, unable to sit any longer.

"Well, as we said earlier, if we end up facing each other this round, I'll give you everything I've got."

Arion rose to look his friend in the eye.

"Good. I'd expect nothing less."

Tybout reached out a hand. They shook hands, the respect clear between them.

Morholt's voice boomed from the entrance of the tent.

"Time for the second round to begin! Squires to the arena!"

The air in the tent shifted. Everyone went silent. Arion and Tybout nodded and headed to the exit.

As they reached the arena, the board for the second round was set. As fate would have it, Arion and Tybout would again avoid facing each other.

Tybout would face a squire named Drest who had won narrowly in the first round by outlasting his opponent. Their battle lasted the longest of all the first-round bouts, and both were exhausted by the end of it. They exchanged blows back and forth, both men refusing to quit. But when the fight finally ended, Drest was the last man standing. He wasn't the strongest fighter but he had resolve.

The massive, blonde, bull-like fighter from the tent's name was Ulrich. He would be facing a fighter named Rowan. Rowan had faced a similar opponent to Ulrich in the first round. He was smaller but proved himself worthy in his first match by using speed and cunning to win.

The brutal fighter from the first round, Leif, was paired with the lone, female fighter left in the melee. Maerwynn showed no emotion when seeing her pairing. And for a solid reason. She had defeated her first round opponent artfully. She moved like water around her foe, using his strikes against him. She put on a master-class of counterstrikes.

Lastly, Arion would face a squire named Renfry.

Renfry was stocky, confident, and clad head-to-toe in black leather. He'd dominated his first opponent with a short sword, honing the weapon like it was an extension of his arm. Arion had learned one thing for certain watching Renfry's first round battle. Renfry rivaled anyone if he were given a sword.

Ulrich and Rowan's match would take place first. The official called them both to the arena.

As they made their way to the arena, Ulrich knocked into Rowan with his shoulder, sneering. Rowan paused for a moment and followed, looking anything but happy.

Ulrich walked to his corner and faced the crowd.

"Rah!!!" he yelled as he pounded his chest and raised his arms. The crowd cheered, eating it up.

Rowan walked confidently to his corner.

An official met them in their corners, handing them their weapons.

Rowan was handed a long pole axe. Bladed on one side, blunted on the other, with a spear point at the tip of the pole. Ulrich was handed a javelin.

Ulrich laughed when he saw his weapon and spun it over in his hand.

The horn sounded.

Ulrich tossed the javelin up and caught it underhand. He quickly lifted it, and flung it full speed at Rowan. Rowan instinctively knocked the javelin to the ground with the butt of his pole axe. Ulrich immediately followed his attack and charged. He had never meant to make contact with Rowan, just distract him so he could get in close where he wanted to fight.

"Smart tactic, I must admit," Arion said quietly to himself.

Rowan was quick enough to see Ulrich's assault, and tried to counter with the blade of the axe. The dulled blade landed cleanly into Ulrich's left shoulder.

The crowd cheered.

Ulrich growled out in pain, but it did not stop his attack. He grabbed the shaft of the axe with his right hand, and forced it from Rowan's hands. He then grabbed the axe and thrust the pole over his knee, snapping it in half. Using the axe portion in his left hand like a typical hand axe and the broken shaft like a club, Ulrich swung wildly like a man possessed. Rowan only had time to throw up his forearms to protect himself.

The crowd gasped loudly as Ulrich continued to beat Rowan until his body went limp.

Ulrich threw down the pieces of the pole axe, and raised his hands to the crowd, roaring loudly. Half of the crowd cheered, while the other silently watched, as the monks raced to aid Rowan. King Mordred beamed as he clapped for the match.

Ulrich was going to the finals.

"He fights without honor. Strength is all he cares about." Tybout whispered to Arion.

"Yeah, and at some point strength won't be enough."

They both watched Ulrich with dislike as he returned to the benches with the other squires. He caught their gaze as he passed them. He grunted uncaringly as he took his place multiple rows behind them.

"Drest!"

"Tybout!"

It was time for Tybout's second round bout.

"Remember he's not the strongest fighter, but if you don't force him in a position to yield, he's not going to quit." Arion reminded Tybout.

Tybout nodded, acknowledging the advice as he watched Drest walk toward the square battlefield. Without saying another word Tybout stood and followed, his eyes steady with focus.

When he reached his corner, Tybout was handed two dirks; short blades, slightly longer than a hunting knife, and Drest was handed a buckler; a small hand shield, and a spear.

Arion couldn't help but go through the strategy in his head.

Tybout's going to have to play this one smart. He will have to close the distance to make those dirks effective. That will be hard to do with the length of that spear.

Tybout must have had the same thoughts, because as soon as the horn sounded he got just outside the reach of the spear, and attempted to flank Drest. Drest was just skilled enough to keep Tybout at reach. Tybout circled Drest again in an attempt to flank him, and again was driven back by the tip of Drest's spear.

Drest decided to go on the offensive. He lunged with his spear and caught Tybout along his ribs, crunching through his leather armor. Tybout instinctively grabbed his side. With Tybout's defenses lowered, Drest slammed his buckler into Tybout's face, throwing him backward.

The crowd let out an "OOO"!

Tybout rolled and landed in a crouch, blood running from his nose and pain flaring in his ribs. He wiped his face, picked up his dirks, and jumped up, back into the fight. Tybout again tried the flanking move, but feinted this time instead of actually attacking. He repeated this multiple more times.

He's not even trying to attack now. He wants to see how he will react. He's setting him up, Arion thought to himself.

Tybout flanked and feinted again. Drest, growing tired of the same sequence over and over again, decided to attack once more.

Drest thrust his spear forward once more.

This was the moment Tybout had been waiting for. The thrust of the spear glanced slightly off his rib cage, as Tybout spun up the shaft of the spear. He had found his way inside the guard of Drest.

He wrapped his arm around the wrist of Drest's spear hand and chopped down hard with his dirk. Drest called out in pain and dropped the spear.

Drest countered by trying to ram the buckler into Tybout. Tybout was quick enough to block the brunt of the blow, but it was still enough to knock him back.

Drest pulled away.

Tybout kicked the spear, knocking it outside of the wooden barriers of the arena. He then charged Drest.

Drest threw a hook with the buckler, using it like a battering ram. Tybout ducked and brought his dirk up, slamming Drest hard in the ribs. Drest cried in pain as he swung the buckler with a back hand, again trying to ram Tybout. Tybout bobbed and sliced again to the other set of ribs. Drest cried out in pain again, this time swinging the buckler with a haymaker. Tybout rolled under the attack again, instead delivering a hard kick to Drest's knee.

Drest dropped to the ground and quickly found the tips of the dirks at his throat.

Drest froze.

"I yield," he muttered, breathless and defeated.

The crowd exploded in applause.

Tybout made it to the final round.

"I've seen great fights, but that was incredible. Your patience, your planning. Great bout!" Arion exclaimed as Tybout returned to the benches, nose still bleeding.

Arion noticed that he was barely out of breath even with all the movement and defensive maneuvers, but saw a slight quiver of pain, hand instinctively reaching toward his ribs as he sat.

"Thanks," Tybout said with a smile. "Once he attacked the first time, I was just trying to draw him out to do it again. If I could get him to attack, I knew I could slip his guard."

"Well, it was great. I'm definitely glad we didn't get paired up against each other," chuckled Arion.

There was now just one more match before Arion's match against Renfry. It was Leif, the cruel fighter from the first round, and Maerwynn, the sole lady left in the contest.

They both made their way to the arena. Leif practically ran to get there. Maerwynn looked calm and poised as she walked. In her corner, she received dual broad axes. Leif received a heavy war hammer, blunted on both ends. The weapons were like a reflection of their personalities.

Tybout whispered to Arion. "This could get ugly."

Arion shook his head. "I don't know. She doesn't seem too worried."

Maerwynn was still strangely calm. Her breathing was rhythmic, almost meditative. Leif, on the other hand, was snorting, and swinging his hammer, eager to induce pain.

The horn sounded.

As expected, Leif charged immediately. He swung the war hammer down with tremendous force. Maerwynn side stepped the attack, moments before he struck. The hammer crashed into the ground so hard that the force could be felt in the stands.

The crowd murmured in response.

Leif shouldered the hammer and surged forward again. Maer-wynn again sidestepped the attack at the last moment.

"She's not trying to strike. She's analyzing him. Looking for a weakness." Arion noted out loud. Tybout nodded in agreement.

Leif, getting frustrated, tried again. This time Maerwynn dodged it but also delivered a counter strike. As the hammer thundered down into the dirt, she slashed one of her axes into his gauntlet. The blow bounced off harmlessly.

"It's going to take more than that, girly." Leif sneered as he prepared for another swing of his hammer. This time he feinted an overhead swing, getting Maerwynn to sidestep once more. Leif countered and changed the angle of his attack. He brought the hammer sideways, swinging like a club. There was no dodging it this time.

The hammer struck Maerwynn directly in the chest.

The crowd gasped as she fell to her knees.

Maerwynn coughed up blood, clutching her chest.

"There it is," Leif said with a cruel smile. "Don't worry. It won't be long now. I'll put you out of your misery, but only because you're a lady, and I'm a gentleman."

He laughed as he swung the hammer once more. Maerwynn tumbled forward, as the hammer crashed into the ground where she knelt moments before.

"I thought she was done for." Tybout gasped.

"Yeah, that was a direct hit. She's tougher than she looks," Arion replied.

Leif grew cocky as he watched her struggle to recover. He began to swing the hammer wildly. Charging and swinging, letting his cruelty and rage take over. Maerwynn, though hurt, still dodged the strikes like a dancer. Leif swung over and over. Frustration began to build with every miss.

"I know I hurt you!" Leif bellowed out in rage. "Let me end the pain! Stay still and fight me!"

Maerwynn tried to show no pain. She just stared at Leif, emotionless and focused, waiting for him to strike again.

Arion then realized. "She's making him burn his energy. Waiting for his attacks to slow."

"You're right! Each swing seems less powerful than the last. Look."

Leif was drenched in sweat. Maerwynn, on the other hand, barely looked as though she had lost her breath.

Leif heaved the hammer over his shoulder once more and charged. He yelled out as he swung the hammer down wildly from over his head. This time instead of sidestepping the attack, Maerwynn stepped forward. She ran one axe into his rib cage and quickly followed the other into his thigh, where it bit into his leather armor effortlessly.

Leif fell to one knee.

The crowd grew silent.

Swarmed with rage, Leif got to his feet and lifted the war hammer.

"I don't care about this contest anymore! I will not be humiliated. Especially by the likes of you! Now, DIE!"

He charged, every other step limping from his bleeding leg. His swing was wild and telegraphed. Maerwynn stood firm, watching his assault. At the last possible moment, she spun toward him, arms outstretched.

She swept across him, spinning like a dancer, her axes flashing in the sun.

One axe knocked the hammer from his hands. The other caught him right at the base of his head with a crack. He dropped to the ground unconscious, blood trickling from his ear.

The match was over.

Maerwynn had won.

Chapter 6: The Swordsman

"Well, guess it's my turn." Arion stood and made his way toward the arena.

"Good luck. Make sure we finish this thing together," Tybout shouted after him.

Renfry stood from the back row of benches and made his way to the square. Arion gazed at Renfry as he turned toward his corner. Renfry caught Arion's eye and gave a respectful nod. Arion returned the gesture politely. Nerves were beginning to build.

In his corner, Arion was handed a short sword and a knife. A perfect pairing. His absolute best combination.

Renfry received a short sword and a shield.

Good. I want him at his best, Arion thought.

Sir Isaac rested his hand on his shoulder. "Remember your stance," he murmured. "And don't let him choose the pace." Arion nodded, confident and ready.

Arion gripped the leather-wrapped hilt of his sword, inhaled deeply, and felt the calm settle into his bones. But then he saw her...

Shyla was walking toward him from the crowd.

"I just wanted to come and say good luck one more time. I know you'll do great," she said. She leaned over the arena fence and kissed him on the cheek.

Arion felt his stomach drop. His face went hot. He managed a nod—maybe a word; he wasn't sure. Shyla was already stepping back, giving him one last bright smile before vanishing into the rising roar of the crowd.

The horn sounded somewhere in the distance.

He didn't notice Renfry charging.

CRACK!

Pain burst from his left arm as Renfry's sword made contact. His arm went limp for a moment, tingling. The pain wrenched him back into reality.

Somewhere behind him, Arion heard Sir Isaac groan into his palms.

"Focus, lad," he muttered under his breath. Arion barely heard it over the throbbing in his arm.

Renfry spun and slammed the shield forward like a battering ram. Arion sprang back just in time, countering with a quick strike. His knife drove into Renfry's shoulder, drawing a muffled growl.

"There he is," Renfry said, lowering his shield with a smirk. "I was wondering when you were going to fight back."

Renfry raised the shield high to guard himself. Arion surged and pressed him relentlessly. He slashed with both blades, forcing Renfry backward step by step until his back hit the arena's corner. Renfry countered.

He came in fast. Much faster than Arion expected. His short sword cut in tight arcs while the shield pressed forward like a bludgeon. Arion dodged the first strike, parried the next, and stepped aside just before the shield smashed into the post behind him with a thundering crack. The wood splintered under the impact. Arion's ribs burned as he tried to catch his breath.

The crowd roared in approval.

Renfry was good.

He fought like someone who had lived his whole life with a blade in hand. Each movement was measured, disciplined, relentless. Every attack flowed into the next. Arion gave ground inch by inch, parrying and dodging. His boots scraped across the packed dirt as he moved.

Renfry pressed harder, shield slamming, blade flashing.

Arion blocked high.

Renfry swept low.

Arion pivoted.

Renfry feinted and caught him again, this time across the ribs.

The breath punched out of him. He staggered.

Renfry circled, confident. "I'll admit, you're good." He sliced his sword through the air. "But I'm better."

Sparks flew as Arion caught the strike with his own sword. Their swords clashed once more.

Arion pressed forward, harder this time, swinging both of his weapons with pinpoint precision and skill. Renfry stepped back, raising the shield in defense. Arion stopped his assault and planted his boot in the middle of the shield, kicking hard. Renfry was knocked back into a post, thrown off balance.

Trapped, Renfry heaved the shield hard at Arion to buy space. Arion sidestepped the wooden missile, dodging it narrowly. Renfry dove behind it, rolled, and struck upward with his sword. Arion reacted quickly. He crossed his short sword and knife, caught the blade in an X, pressed it down to the hilt... and twisted.

The torque wrenched the hilt sideways, forcing the sword from Renfry's grip.

Arion kicked him square in the chest and stood over him, blades poised inches from Renfry's face.

"I yield," Renfry muttered.

The crowd roared.

He had won. He reached down a hand in respect, helping Renfry to his feet.

The horns blared triumphantly as Arion finally let out a deep breath. Shyla was on her feet somewhere in the crowd, cheering, though Arion couldn't see her through the haze of adrenaline. All he felt was the hum of victory, an ache in his ribs, and the shooting pain in his left arm. He had just earned his place among the final four.

He didn't have long to celebrate his victory.

As Arion stepped back toward the bench, the cheers shifted. A ripple moved through the stands. A murmur of excitement, confusion... anticipation.

Morholt strode into the arena, raising his arms for silence.

"Congratulations to our four champions!" he boomed. "But hear me well, young squires. Becoming a knight of Camelot is not so simple as besting another squire."

Arion's stomach tightened.

"For as tradition demands," Morholt continued, "those who wish to earn the title of Sabaton Knight must face one final test. A trial of unity, valor, and unmatched skill."

The crowd roared.

Arion exchanged nervous glances with the other three victors.

"Prepare yerselves," Morholt said, grinning. "Your final challenger awaits." Morholt turned, arm outstretched, and gestured to the warrior.

A shadow stepped into the arena behind him. A figure clad in dark armor, a crested helmet, and a stance unmistakably lethal.

A full-fledged Sabaton Knight.

Arion felt his heartbeat jump.
One final battle.

Chapter 7: The Final Trial

Tybout, Ulrich, and Maerwynn made their way to the square to join Arion. For the final trial, the squires were able to choose a weapon from the rack. The three others quickly made their choice of weapons. Ulrich grabbed a massive zweihander sword, nearly six feet long and wide as a tree trunk. It would have crushed any normal person.

Tybout grabbed the combination that Arion had in his second round match: a short sword and a knife.

Maerwynn grabbed a set of estocs and flashed them in a quick twirl in her hands.

Arion walked to the rack and grabbed a simple arming sword.It was nearly three feet long and felt exceptionally balanced in his hand. With this weapon he could wield it with one or two hands, which would allow him to move well, using his speed as a weapon.

Arion looked at the others. "Alright, our best chance is to work together. This is a fully trained warrior."

"I agree. We don't want to take any chances," Tybout replied.

Maerwynn nodded in agreement.

"Just stay out of my way," Ulrich barked as he walked toward his corner.

The others exchanged looks, but quickly turned their attention to the knight.

The Sabaton Knight stood directly in the center of the arena, brandishing an iron shield and a long-shafted glaive; hooked on one side and bladed on the other. He was defended from all angles between his armor and the iron shield. Using the glaive, he could keep the squires at bay with his long reach. Even in the close quarters he wielded it skillfully.

Arion looked at Tybout and Maerwynn. "He's too well defended to make a direct assault. We are going to have to take turns attacking and hope that one of us can strike while he's focused on the other."

Maerwynn nodded. "I'll strike first. You follow."

Tybout and Arion shook their heads in agreement.

The officials then led them to their corners.

This time, the nerves were present. Arion took a deep breath, but he could still feel his hand trembling slightly. This was not going to be a simple fight. The others seemed to have the same thoughts as they looked around at each other. They each nodded, ready for the round to begin.

On cue, the horn sounded.

They stepped forward, ready to attack as planned.

Ulrich, however, had his own ideas.

He charged at full speed and swung his massive sword at the knight. The knight simply blocked the blow with his shield. The metal clanged together so loudly that it stunned the others. Spectators covered their ears until the ringing faded from the square. Ulrich gathered himself and stepped back.

"Well, that didn't work," he grunted. "I'll give him that. He's strong."

Arion and the others shook off the disorientation and quickly began to encircle the knight, just out of reach of his glaive. The knight slowly backed himself into a corner against the wooden barrier of the ring. He was strong and clever. As long as he stayed against the barrier, they would have no choice but to attack from the front.

Maerwynn charged, as planned. She advanced quickly; he countered just as quickly. He swung the glaive around in a sweeping arc. She jumped and dodged the swipe, flipping her hips overhead, and struck with both estocs along his helm.

The estocs rang sharply off his helm, jolting his neck, and clanged annoyingly loud in his ears. He turned his attention toward her as she jumped back out of his reach, clutching her chest; her injury from earlier flaring beneath her armor.

Arion didn't wait for him to bring his defenses back to center. He lunged and drove his sword forward. The dull blade would not penetrate the armor, but the strike rattled the knight and left a shallow crease in the metal.

The knight cried out in pain and frustration before quickly resetting himself against the barrier.

Tybout dove at him from the side before he could fully set, but the knight again showed his quickness. This time swinging the iron shield wide and bashing it into Tybout's face.

Tybout flew back, his short sword flung from his hand as he hit the ground. He got up quickly, blood running freely from his nose.

"Again!?" Tybout complained, as he wiped the blood running over his lips.

They continued to strike in this pattern for a short while; one would charge, and the others would attempt to strike while the knight was focused elsewhere. After repeated failed attempts and all of them drenched in sweat, Arion took a step back.

"This isn't working. We need a new approach."

Arion winced as he straightened, a sharp pulse flaring across his bruised ribs. His left arm tingled in and out with feeling, as he breathed deeply, trying to catch his breath.

"I'm sick of this! I'm ending it!" Ulrich yelled suddenly, and again charged alone. The knight was quicker this time. He swung with his glaive catching Ulrich's zweihander with the hook, and yanked hard. Ulrich tripped forward and the knight thrashed the shield directly into his head. A sickening crack echoed through the arena. The crowd hushed. Ulrich was out cold.

Monks rushed to the arena and carried off his limp body.

"Like I said," Arion muttered, "we need a new plan." He looked at the remaining two, hoping one had a strategy. They looked back, both exhausted and concerned. Arion looked around the arena, searching for an answer.

It came to him as he scanned the wooden planks surrounding them.

"If he wants to use the boundary to keep us from getting behind him... then we remove the boundary... Keep him busy!"

The other two still looked puzzled, but they nodded. They began feinting attacks toward the knight. Each time, getting just close enough to force him to defend, but always jumping back out of reach.

Arion quickly set to work with his plan. He grabbed his arming sword with both hands and struck down hard at the wooden barrier. Each downward strike sent a jolt up his sore arm, but he gritted his teeth and swung again. He struck again and again until the boards splintered, finally breaking.

It didn't take long for the knight to realize what was happening. For the first time in the fight he was forced to advance. If he could reposition along another barrier, he could reset his defense. The squires were determined to prevent it. The crowd began to cheer, sensing the fight was about to turn.

"Attack! Now!" Arion yelled.

Maerwynn winced as she charged, ignoring the pain in her chest, attacking as she did earlier. To her surprise, the knight used the same defensive tactic again, this time out of position. She jumped and launched her aerial assault. Tybout managed to get behind him, with the barrier removed, as the knight focused on the overhead strike.

The knight raised his shield to block the estocs and whipped the glaive pole backward toward Tybout. He succeeded in knocking Tybout back, turning as he did so. Maerwynn's attack glanced harmlessly off his shield. She rolled away, one hand briefly brushing the spot where the hammer had struck her, masking her anguish.

The knight did not have enough time to react to Arion, who slid in from the opposite side, ribs screaming in protest, and swept his blunted sword low. Both of the knight's heavy knees buckled. The impact jarred his entire frame, his shield fell from his grip as he whipped toward the ground.

He barely caught himself on the shaft of the glaive, moments before his armor collided with the earth. Now bent on all fours, he tried to rise, but the three squires quickly surrounded him, weapons steady and ready to strike. He looked around realizing that he could not rise before being struck, and bowed his head.

The Sabaton Knight slammed his free hand into the ground, and then laughed breathlessly.

"I yield. Well fought. All of you."

The horn sounded, marking the end of the battle.

The arena erupted.

Chapter 8: The Prize

Sir Morholt came to greet the three remaining squires.

"'Ello again. Seems you three have earned the right to stand beside me. 'Tis a great honor. One that many only dream of. To become part of the brotherhood is a blessing indeed. We welcome you with open arms." He beamed at the three of them proudly. "Next, you will each get to meet the Lords and the King himself during the knighting ceremony. Afterwards, you will each get to take your turn with the lance outside."

All three murmured in excitement. Meeting the King, and moreover, taking their chance at the Lance of King Arthur was an opportunity beyond what any of them had ever imagined.

"Now, a couple of things," Morholt continued. "First, the King does not take well to any sort of impoliteness, so be honorable as I know you are, and you'll do fine. Second, while I understand the excitement of tryin' to pull out the lance, don't go strainin' yourself tryin' ter yank out the bloody thing. All have tried. None have succeeded. The legend says that only someone of Arthur's bloodline can remove it. Arthur left no kin, no children. It's really just for sport." He tapped the side of his helm. "Lastly, once you have all been officially knighted and you've finished with the lance, return here. You'll receive your post and training plan. King Mordred himself will decide where he needs each one of you and you will travel there tomorrow."

All three nodded in understanding.

"I shall return for you momentarily, when the King is ready," Morholt said, disappearing from the tent.

Arion turned to the other two, at last.

"Great job! We're going to make a great team," he said, smiling.

Tybout looked at him and smiled. "I'm glad we made it here together." He stuck out his hand. Arion returned the gesture.

Maerwynn looked at them and smiled. "I'm honored to stand beside you both. You are both great warriors."

At the far end of the tent, Ulrich was stuffing his gear into his bag with angry, jerking movements. His head was bandaged and he had dried blood down the side of his face from his ear. He stormed toward them. His steps were uneven, but fury kept him upright.

"Thanks to you, I won't get that honor." His glare locked directly onto Arion. "You wanted to be the leader. You should've gone first... you coward. It should be me, gettin' to pull that lance out. It should be me, being knighted. Not you wimps."

He spat at the dirt and stormed out.

Arion, Tybout, and Maerwynn exchanged glances but shrugged it off. Their excitement quickly returned as they talked through the battles and wondered aloud where they might be posted.

Morholt reappeared, voice suddenly serious.
"It is time. Follow me."

Morholt led the three warriors out into the courtyard where the statues stood. Waiting for them were the five Brothers of Lot and the winners of the other competitions, which included Shyla.

King Mordred sat apart from his brothers on his black and gold throne. His cold obsidian eyes swept over the former squires.

Arion and the others joined the line. Mordred looked to his brothers, nodded, and rose from his throne.

"Welcome to the knighting ceremony!" Mordred declared, voice booming through the courtyard. "These ten squires have completed the trials necessary to join my illustrious army. The last step of their journey is to be knighted by my hand. Each will come forth. My sword will be placed upon their shoulders and each will recite the Code of Honor."

He looked at each of the squires, his gaze as cold as ice. "Come forward each of you and swear your allegiance to my kingdom, and join the brotherhood."

Mordred raised his obsidian blade, *Sceaduwe*, to a roar of cheers.

One by one, each knelt. Arion's ribs tightened painfully as he dropped to one knee. Together they repeated the words of the oath:

"I swear to serve the liege lord in valor,
To live by honor and by glory,
To guard the honor of the King,
To never refuse a challenge of an equal,
To never turn my back upon any foe,
To be loyal to the King,
And to protect the Kingdom until my last breath."

Mordred then stood over them, placing his blade on their shoulder.

Arion felt a lifeless cold wash over him as the black blade touched each of his shoulders. *That is one sword I hope to never have to feel the wrath of,* he thought.

As he rose, he noticed the King staring at him, staring at his pendant. Mordred's face was slowly becoming twisted, almost hateful. They made eye contact for just a moment before King Mordred turned and walked back to his throne.

He shot a look of death at Arion before addressing the crowd.

Arion couldn't help but feel like he had done something very wrong.

"Stand, young knights! Be proud of all you have accomplished!"

The courtyard erupted. Arion spotted the monk clapping excitedly, next to Sir Isaac. A moment later, he found Shyla's eye from the other end of the line. She grinned, and he quickly returned his gaze to the ground, warmth flushing his face.

Mordred continued, "Now we will make our way to the fields for our little sport. Each of our new knightlings will get an attempt to pull the infamous lance of my dear uncle from the ground. This is a prized possession of the Pendragon family, and what gave my uncle his claim to the throne."

His voice darkened.

"Should any of you succeed in removing it… I would consider it an immediate threat to my reign… we will settle the matter. *Haha!*"

He forced a laugh as he spoke. The glare that followed it made it very clear that it wasn't truly a joke. The crowd murmured nervously at his words. Arion swore the King shot him a look of pure venom before he turned back to the crowd.

"Let us go!"

The crowd surged with excitement, spilling out of the castle walls, toward the fields where the Kings' War took place so many years before.

Arion and the other new knights were ushered to the teal pole, the lance of King Arthur. The ropes surrounding it had now been removed. The crowd circled around them, buzzing with anticipation.

Shyla was called to attempt first. She walked up to the lance, wrapped both hands around the long shaft, and pulled with her entire might.

Nothing.

The pole did not bend, the ground did not move.

She tried once more.

Nothing. Not a grain of dirt moved.

She finally let go, curtsied to the crowd, and stepped beside Arion.

The crowd clapped politely.

"Guess I'm not a king," Shyla said, with a small smile, shrugging her shoulders.

Arion chuckled. "No, I guess not. I'd wager thousands have tried over the years and none have moved it any more than you."

"Probably true." She laughed. "Besides, I think it should remain here anyway, a tribute to King Arthur."

"Well, *I* wouldn't want to be the one that pulls it free," Arion whispered. "King Mordred was deadly serious when he said he would take it as a threat to his reign. Even if he tried to make a joke of it."

Shyla giggled. "I would not worry too much. You don't look very kingly anyhow."

Together they watched as each new knight gave it their best attempt. The lance didn't so much as twitch.

Tybout took his turn. Nothing.

Maerwynn. Nothing.

Soon, only Arion and two others remained. Sir Isaac moved through the crowd to stand at Arion's side.

Sir Morholt called him forward. His feet stood rooted to the ground as he looked over the crowd, all staring at him eagerly. Sir Isaac nudged him forward.

For reasons he couldn't explain, Arion felt more nervous here than he had the entire tournament. A sword in his hand and blood pumping felt natural. This didn't. Having all eyes on him, especially *Mordred's*, it seemed like a world of pressure.

As he approached the lance, he saw King Mordred hush one of his brothers as he locked his eyes on Arion. He leaned forward in his throne.

Arion heard him whisper, "This one..."

Heart pounding, Arion stepped up to the teal shaft glinting in the setting sun. The ground around it was darker than the surrounding soil—still charred years later.

Arion took one final look at the many faces staring back at him. He could feel King Mordred's gaze but avoided eye contact with him. He found the old monk again. When they met eyes, the old monk gave him a small smile and nodded reassuringly.

Arion took a deep breath, still unsure why he felt so nervous. His arm throbbed as he reached for the lance.

Small jolts of electricity sparked around his hand as it wrapped around the metal pole. His pulse spiked. The air thickened.

From the corner of his eye, he saw King Mordred take a step forward.

Arion placed his second hand on the shaft.

Thunder clapped through the blue sky above. Dark clouds formed, materializing from nowhere. Claps of thunder followed lightning that seemed to jump from cloud to cloud.

Lightning crawled over his arms, spiraling around him like living veins of light. The hair on his arms rose. Little sparks of lightning crept across his armor.

The crowd stumbled back. The muffled gasps and screams could barely be heard over the crackling of the electricity. The monk stood motionless, eyes fixed on Arion. Gawain had gone still, eyes widening. Agravain rose halfway from his seat, hands on his blade. Gareth muttered a curse under his breath, while Gaheris stared unblinking. Mordred glared at Arion, confusion, shock, and anger coming in waves across his face.

Arion pulled.

The lance slid from its stony place in the earth as effortlessly as a blade through parchment.

The sky answered in another violent crack of thunder. Lightning surged wildly around him, the lance sparking madly, then the lightning was sucked inward, into his body. Only faint sparks crackled and sparked where his hand held firmly onto the lance.

The world froze.

Then…

"SEIZE HIM! SEIZE THAT LANCE!" Mordred shrieked. "I will not be challenged! I am your king! The *rightful* king!"

The courtyard erupted into chaos.

Chapter 9: The Escape

"Seize him! I knew there was something… familiar about him! He cannot get away!" King Mordred roared as his Sabaton Guard surged forward. The Brothers of Lot scrambled to their feet, weapons drawn, awaiting their king's orders.

Arion barely had time to process what was happening. His pulse was racing. His hands trembled around the mystical lance. Without knowing how or why, lightning burst from the tip of the lance in an explosion of energy and power. Mordred's Sabaton Guard hurled backwards like rag dolls.

The crowd screamed and began to scatter, running for the castle walls.

Through the chaos, four figures sprinted toward Arion. Shyla, her bow already nocked and drawn, eyes blazing with determination. Tybout, curved knives flashing in each hand; Maerwynn, with a single estoc twirling like the wind; and lastly, Sir Isaac, his old tattered sword, steady in his hand.

They fell into formation beside Arion without hesitation.

Mordred's voice cut through the confusion like a blade: "If he gets away, I will have your heads! I must know who he is! Brothers! Arm your men!" The brothers fell back and began to organize their men.

The Sabaton Guard staggered to their feet again, regaining their formation. Arion braced himself, gripping *Ron* in his uninjured arm. A firm hand clamped down on his shoulder.

The monk—now bearing two short swords.

And for the first time, Arion understood that flicker of familiarity in the courtyard earlier that day.

"Come this way!" the monk commanded. "We must escape to the woods while we have time. There we will be hidden."

Arion didn't question it. He turned and sprinted. "Come on!" he shouted back.

Shyla and Tybout followed.

"Go! I will hold them here!" yelled Sir Isaac.

"I will stay here with your knight. We will slow them down. Go...Now!" Maerwynn insisted.

Arion watched as the two charged into the horde of knights following Mordred's orders. In a flash of silver steel they battled, until Arion could no longer see them. Lost in a sea of enemies.

The four of them ran as soldiers began to pour from the castle walls. Charger and Sabaton Knights flooded the open field after them. Shyla loosed arrows with deadly precision, dropping one soldier, then another. Tybout and the monk slashed through others as they passed.

Arion barely had time to think. Instinctively, lightning rained from *Ron* in crackling arcs that sent armored men sprawling or running for their lives.

Then—a large mass collided with Tybout, knocking him clean off his feet.

Arion skidded to a stop, instinctively turning back. The mass was Ulrich, who was getting to his feet. Arion was about to charge when Tybout jumped up with a mischievous grin.

"Don't worry about me! Go! I've been itching to fight this ogre since the tournament. Seems I'll get my chance now!"

He lunged at Ulrich, blades flashing. Charger Knights began closing in around them.

"Hurry up with him, and meet us in the woods!" Arion called. Tybout gave him a nod and smiled, slicing his blades at Ulrich.

It was the last time he would get a nod from Tybout. Moments later, a Charger Knight launched a spear from atop his steed.

Tybout's body went limp instantly.

"NOO!" Arion screamed. A cold weight settled into his chest as he watched his friend fall.

The monk grabbed him again by the shoulder. "Come. We are running out of time."

Mordred and a company of Charger Knights were already thundering toward them, closing the distance with each moment.

Arion tore himself away and sprinted toward the woods, his ribs burning as he ran.

Shyla and the monk were nearing the edge of the woods as he finally caught up with them, all breathing hard.

The monk stopped abruptly and turned.

"Arion, we will not escape without your use of *Ron,*" he said, gesturing toward the lance.

Arion looked at the lance, the golden dragon wings at the tip still crackling with power.

"But I don't know how," Arion said, breathless and trembling. "Everything that's happened so far…wasn't me. It just…happened."

The monk softened his tone.

"Then stop thinking. Feel. Find your heartbeat. The lance responds to the bloodline that carries Arthur's spark."

Behind them, hooves pounded closer. Mordred and his company flooded toward the trees.

"Focus," the monk said, trying to remain calm. "Ignore all else. Just listen."

Arion closed his eyes. He breathed deeply and focused his mind.

Thump…thump.

Thump…thump.

Thump. Thump.

Power pulsed into his palms. Heat surged through *Ron.*

Lightning erupted in a roaring wave before them. When he opened his eyes there was a wall of lightning separating them from Mordred's squadron. Arion dropped to his knees, exhaustion overcoming him.

Mordred shrieked in frustration.

"Nooo! You cannot run from me! Tell me who you are! Arthur had no son. I was his only son! How do you possess that weapon? The Pendant—where did you get that pendant!?"

Arion couldn't speak. His mind raced with thoughts and questions of his own.

The monk stepped forward.

"You do not need to come find us, Dark King. We will find you, in time. Until then, know this…there were secrets of Arthur's that even I did not know, until now."

"Don't speak to me, old man!" Mordred spat. "You know nothing of my uncle. And you know nothing of my wrath. But you shall. Very soon!"

The monk rolled back his sleeve to reveal a tattoo. A circle and the Roman numeral II on top of crossed swords. Arion recognized it as the same symbol as the one on his pendant. He grabbed the pendant and looked down at it. His pendant had numeral I, while the monk was inked with the numeral II.

His voice rose, echoing through the clearing.

"Oh, I know your wrath all too well. And I knew your uncle more intimately than you could imagine. I was his right hand...and I failed him."

He stepped into the light.

"I have hidden for far too long in shame. But my time in the shadows is over. It is time the world remembers me."

His eyes were fierce now, alive again, as they once were.

"It is I...Lancelot!"

Mordred stared in disbelief. Rage twisted visibly on his face. He tried to speak but could not find the words. His world was unraveling.

Before he could recover, Lancelot seized Arion's arm, grabbed Shyla's wrist, and yanked them both deeper into the woods.

They vanished into the trees as Mordred regained his voice and screamed orders behind them in the distance.

Chapter 10: The Monk

They ran deeper and deeper into the forest, branches whipping past them, roots threatening to trip their exhausted legs. After what seemed like hours, the shouting behind them faded. They could no longer hear hooves thundering against the earth. Mordred's voice was silenced.

The sun was fully set, and the night sky flickered between the gaps in the branches above them. At last, the monk lifted a hand, signaling them to stop.

"I believe we have distanced ourselves enough for the night," he said, breathing hard.

Arion stopped and dropped to his knees, exhausted. His ribs burned with each breath. Suddenly a flood of emotion came over him. He punched the ground in rage. Tears flowed freely down his cheeks.

"They're dead, aren't they? All of them!"

"That is the most likely outcome. Yes," the monk replied solemnly, his voice steady, but something in his eyes said he'd had this conversation with himself a hundred times.

Arion cried harder. Shyla fell to the ground to comfort him.

"It's all my fault! Maerwynn, Isaac, Tybout – they all died to protect me. I should have saved them!" He began to pound the ground harder. He punched repeatedly until his arms became numb and his knuckles were raw and bloodied. His damaged arm stung worse than before, but he did not care. He stayed there kneeling, breathing heavily, wincing in pain, until he finally started to gather himself. His breath slowed and the tears stopped. He looked at the monk. "What happened back there? Why did King Mordred chase me?"

The monk just stared back at him. Sorrow showed deeply in his eyes, but he replied with little emotion.

"Let's make a camp here for the night. I will tell you everything I know."

Shyla looked at him. "I don't know what's going on either, but I do know that none of them were forced to do what they did. They chose to, and they would do it again if given the chance. Just like I would."

She hugged him and then stood up. She reached out a hand to help him to his feet. He nodded in thanks and they set out to gather firewood in silence.

After some time, Arion, Shyla, and the monk had a small fire burning. They warmed themselves and cooked two small animals they had caught along the way. The woods hummed softly around them.

Arion sat staring into the flames, thoughts swirling in his head. He looked up at the monk, unable to hold his tongue any longer.

"I...I'm sorry, but did I hear you correctly back there? You...you're Lancelot?"

Lancelot nodded. "Aye, I'm sorry I have kept my identity hidden. But I had to be certain you were who I believed you to be. I could not risk revealing myself before it was confirmed."

Arion blinked. "Confirmed? Confirmed what?"

"That you are the legacy of the Pendragon." Lancelot said gently. "That you are the son of King Arthur."

Arion's stomach did a flip. His thoughts crashed and scattered. Shyla stared between them in utter fascination.

Before Arion could gather himself, Shyla burst in with a flurry of questions:

"Wait, I thought Lancelot was dead?"

"Arthur and Guinevere didn't have a son did they? How could he be Arthur's?"

"How *did* he pull the Lance from the stone?"

"Arion, who is your mother? Is...wait...*is your mother Guinevere?!*"

Lancelot chuckled softly. "Slow down. I will answer all of this in time. First, I assure you, I am not dead. I am very clearly alive and well. As for the rest..."

He sighed, the sorrow in his eyes now returned, showing in the firelight.

"Arion, many years ago I served as your father's right hand. It was my duty to protect both him and our kingdom. During our travels in Rome, he confided in me that there was one other woman he had loved beyond Guinevere. He met her during our wars with the Gauls. A woman he never intended to love, but love rarely listens to intention."

He paused, letting the words settle.

"He admitted to me that they shared one night together before he left her behind, because she was not of noble blood. No one knew of this but myself...and perhaps Merlin.

This woman was your mother, Elaine."

Arion felt his jaw drop lower with every sentence. Lancelot continued, his voice becoming thick with guilt.

"The night Arthur fell..." he paused, as though reliving the night over in his head. "I was tasked with fleeing with Guinevere.

But I became cut off. She escaped with other Knights of the Round Table. I instead continued the fight inside the castle. When I heard Arthur had died, I fled through the secret passageways of the castle. I rode blindly without looking back and eventually wound up in the sacred city of Dunholm. In my shame, I vowed my services to the monks, believing I had failed my king and queen.

Shyla and Arion sat frozen, listening, watching as Lancelot's tears reflected in the fire.

"It was only when I received a letter, about a boy who fought like a born warrior from South Hamtun, that I gained hope. The way you were described; your skill, your looks, your age...it all matched Arthur's timeline. I knew Elaine lived there. From that moment, I suspected the truth."

He took a deep, slow breath.

"I had to see for myself. I visited South Hamtun a number of times just to see if my hunch was correct, watching you from a distance. The older you became, the more I knew. I influenced Sir Isaac where I could, ensuring your training continued. I needed today to confirm what I believed in my heart. First, I saw the pendant that hangs from your neck. And then the Lance. Once you removed it from the earth, I knew then for certain."

Arion's head spun. This old monk was the famous Lancelot? His father, King Arthur?

It felt impossible. He looked down at the pendant, wondering how much his mother knew.

As though Lancelot were reading his mind, he continued quietly, "Your mother stayed silent to protect you. King Mordred would have had you killed as a babe if he knew you carried Arthur's blood. With every breath you take, you challenge him.

He claims the throne because he killed your father, but if the world learns Arthur had an heir...Mordred's rule collapses."

Lancelot leaned forward.

"We must continue to the North. There we can hide while I hone your abilities. You will learn to wield *Ron,* so that you may take on the Brothers of Lot. To gather allies and strength. And when the time is right, to claim the throne. To claim your birthright, and return the kingdom to what it once was."

Arion surged to his feet. Rage trembled through him.

"Claim *my* throne? What throne? I never knew him! How can I be owed any of this? He never visited me. Not once. He never claimed me. And who says I want this?"

His voice cracked.

"I didn't ask for any of this. I just wanted to be a knight. Before this morning, I barely knew that the Kingdom was even this dark. And now suddenly I'm supposed to believe I'm some chosen heir because I pulled an enchanted stick from the ground?!"

He hurled the Lance, *Ron,* to the ground. Electricity and sparks crackled as it bounced, the ground now scorched where it lay.

Lancelot stood calmly. "I know this is a lot to take on. No one expects you to bear this alone. Fate may have named you, but we will shape your path together. You will not do this alone. I will train you."

He nodded toward Shyla.

"And I believe Miss Shyla here plans to stand with you."

Shyla flushed, then met Arion's eyes.

"I do. Arion...I knew there was something different the moment we met. I saw it the moment you stood before that stone. I saw power, yes. But more than that, I saw kindness. That's why the lance chose you. That's why I chose you."

She stepped forward and took his hand.

"And together, we will face the Brothers of Lot."

Arion looked away, conflicted. "I can feel the power surge through me when I hold the lance."

"Its name is *Ron,*" Lancelot interjected.

"Okay, when I hold *Ron*. But that doesn't make it any easier to believe. I'm just a squire from South Hamtun. I'm not a royal. I've never known anything other than fishing piers and my sword. How can I be the heir to Camelot?"

Lancelot rose and placed both hands on Arion's shoulders

"No one expects you to understand it all tonight. This is much to take in. But pulling *Ron* from the stone confirms the truth. In time, you will believe it too. For now, it's getting late. We should get some sleep. In the morning, we continue our way north. We will be protected in Dunholm, at least for a time."

They doused the fire and lay beneath the canopy.

Arion's thoughts churned in his head long after the flames died out. He turned and noticed Shyla watching him, eyes warm, hopeful. She smiled softly before rolling over.

Eventually, the whispering branches above blurred into darkness, and sleep finally claimed him.

Chapter 11: The Archer

Lancelot had insisted they sleep in shifts. Shyla had volunteered for the first watch. Arion was softly snoring next to her. Lancelot sat motionless, leaning against a log, not fully asleep but not awake. Shyla could see the tension in his stance—he was listening to every sound.

She replayed all that she had witnessed and heard over in her mind. She was lying next to one of the most famous and respected knights in the kingdom. She was also mere feet away from the son of King Arthur. The more she tried to consider it, the more it seemed unreal. But she had watched Arion pull the lance from the ground. She had tried with all her own strength to move it and it did not budge. He had removed it effortlessly. Lightning had called to him and he answered with his name.

She looked again at Lancelot and stared for a moment. *If only her father could have been there with her.*

Her father was an archer in the Knights of the Round Table. He fought alongside Arthur's men in the Kings' War. When Arthur fell, fearing for his family, he laid down his honor and vowed allegiance to Mordred. But he never became fully loyal.

In Bristow, he taught her in secret, the code of the Knights of the Round Table. He told her stories of the old days and how the Kingdom thrived under King Arthur. He taught her how to use a bow. They would spend hours hunting in the woods fine-tuning her accuracy, strength, and dexterity.

"A kingdom is not built by crowns, Shy... but by those willing to stand against evil and protect the innocent."

She could hear his voice as she remembered the words in her head.

He led a secret society called "The Order". They trained in secret with plans to rise up against the Brothers of Lot and their oppressive rule. The Order was small but grew larger as the years went on. Apparently too large. One night her father left to meet with The Order. He never returned.

On the night of one of The Order's meetings, the barn where they met was set on fire. Mordred's men were seen marching toward the barn's location earlier that evening. When the barn was found the next day, there were no survivors. Mordred had caught wind of the treason and had ordered them to be eradicated.

Shyla remembered the tears falling from her face as she stared at the charred remains of the barn. The unrecognizable bodies among the wreckage. The only proof she had that her father was there, was his bow, left unscathed in the tall grass nearby. The bow she still carried with her now. It was all she had left of her father.

This was the real reason she had spent the next few years training to become a Ranger Knight. To honor her father and to carry out his plan; to kill Mordred. But during the trials something happened that she had not expected. She met Arion.

The way he blushed when she first met him. The way he fought so skillfully in the trials, like he was defending his family. And how he was so humble. He had not wanted *Ron* even moments before he took his turn. But then he pulled *Ron* from the ground.

Mordred's reaction and fear was more than she could have asked for. The moment he pulled *Ron* from the ground, she knew. Her father had died in the hope that this day would happen. Arion was the beginning of everything he dreamed.

She looked at Arion, his face softly lit by the moonlight as he slept.

"He doesn't even want any of this…," she muttered quietly, as she watched him breathe deeply. "But they will hunt him to all corners of Britain."

In her head she could hear her father's voice once more. *"Shy, a true knight stands for all that is good. When we find the good in life we must protect it at all costs."*

She wiped the tears running down her cheeks, and whispered to Arion, "My father died believing in King Arthur. In you. Lancelot says you are Arthur's son, so I will stand with you until my final breath. I swear on his bow and his blood, I will not fail you, as this kingdom failed him."

The bow shone in the moonlight next to her as she finally slipped away into sleep.

Chapter 12: The Mage

"Wake up. We must move." Lancelot was already awake and packed. The sun was just beginning to peek over the horizon. "They will be still looking for us. We must head north."

They traveled through the forest until nearly midday when the trees finally thinned and a clearing opened before them. A small trade town sat inside a low log wall, its gates propped open as merchants and travelers drifted in and out. Soldiers guarded the entrance. Their cloaks were marked with the banner of Gareth, Lord of the North: a red boar rearing on its hind legs over a black shield.

"Put your hoods up," Lancelot whispered. "Strap your weapons. We are weary travelers, nothing more. Speak to no one and keep your heads down. We cannot risk being recognized."

They strapped their weapons and hid them beneath their cloaks as they passed the gate slowly. The guards wore fur-lined mail and had harsh northern features, their eyes like winter ice. None of the guards paid them any attention as they entered. They slipped into the town unnoticed.

"This is the trade town of Ledes." Lancelot spoke low to avoid wandering eyes. "It is an open village to all travelers. But be wary…the town, like all of the north, is watched by Lord Gareth. He is the youngest of King Mordred's brothers. He was once compassionate, righteous even…now, he is known for his ruthlessness. The cold of the north seems to have affected his heart. Sadly, it just shows that power and fear can change any man."

They found a cookshop and slid into a table in the back, hoping to hear if news of the events in Camelot had traveled this far north. They kept their hoods low as they ate, pretending to be nothing more than travelers resting their feet. Arion flexed his sore knuckles as they sat. The swelling had worsened. Soldiers and knights came and went, the air thick with noise and warmth from the fire.

A group of knights and soldiers sat near the entrance enjoying themselves off duty. They were loud and boisterous as they drank and ate. They laughed and spoke of raids and rumors of Gareth's raising of pay to soldiers. But nothing of Camelot, or Arion, or anything that made them think news had reached Ledes yet.

One knight was not drinking and parading about like the others. He had watched as Arion, Shyla, and Lancelot entered the shop. He sat still, intently watching them as those around him remained blissfully unaware, too deep in drink and laughter to notice anything out of the ordinary.

Shyla leaned close, keeping her gaze low. "There's a knight who keeps glancing our way." She motioned toward the knight, who had still not removed his gaze.

"Do nothing out of the ordinary," Lancelot warned. "We finish our meal, then leave."

"I don't think that will be an option." Shyla muttered.

The knight stood. He made his way toward them, table by table. His hand slowly drifted toward his sword as he moved nearer. His eyes were locked on them.

"If he draws his blade," Lancelot whispered, "you two run out the back. I will hold them off."

The knight was only a couple of paces away now.

He began to unsheathe his sword...

BOOM!

The cookshop shook violently, dust falling from the rafters as a thunderous explosion rocked the courtyard outside.

"All soldiers outside!" a decorated Sabaton Knight called out.

The knight approaching them had stopped, and spun toward the door. He ran out with the others, to see what had caused the explosion.

"Go," Lancelot said sharply. "Out the back. Do not run, but make haste."

They slipped out the backdoor, unseen through the chaos. Following Lancelot, they ran behind the rows of shops and buildings that lined the courtyard. Through gaps in the buildings, Arion saw the cause of the madness. There were shattered wooden barrels, spilled grain, and chicken feathers floating like snow. Patches of purple flame littered the ground, dancing as people ran for safety. Soldiers scrambled in every direction, barking orders for people to return indoors and for the culprit to reveal themselves and surrender.

As they ran, distancing themselves from the mayhem, Arion noticed a small barn, near the back gates of Ledes.

"Lancelot! Look over there! We can hide in there until things calm down."

"Great idea. Move!"

They entered the barn and threw themselves onto the hay-laden floor. They sat trying to catch their breath and gather themselves. For a moment they rested, until Shyla stiffened.

"Uh...guys." She nodded toward the rafters.

A pair of purple eyes stared back at them, glowing in the dim light of the barn.

They sprang to their feet, weapons drawn.

"Come down," Shyla warned. "Or I'll put an arrow through your heart."

Chicken feathers dropped slowly from the rafters as a lanky boy lowered himself down. More feathers shed from his clothes as he landed in a crouch.

"Don't kill me!" he blurted. "The fire was accidental...mostly. I meant no harm."

He was younger than both Arion and Shyla. He had jet black curly hair that grew wildly over his eyes. But his eyes stood out most. He had electric purple eyes, the same color as the flames in the street. His tunic was patchy and tattered, chicken feathers sticking out of holes in the fabric. A small satchel hung over his shoulder, its flap embroidered with a rune. The satchel looked as if it had been charred more than once.

Despite his disheveled appearance, there was an undeniable spark to him—a restless, fidgeting energy. His fingers twitched as though they would explode with power at any moment and he kept shifting his weight like magic might burst out of him if he sneezed.

His voice cracked. He tried to sound braver than he felt.

"I didn't mean to blow up the grain. Or the chickens. Or the...well...everything. My magic just does what it wants sometimes."

His glowing eyes darted over Arion, Shyla, and Lancelot, widening when they fell on *Ron*.

"That weapon...it hums with energy. I can feel it from here," he whispered.

He stared at each of them, weighing something silently, then swallowed hard.

"Right. So…uh…hello. I'm Van, and I know I'm in trouble."

He hesitated, then added with a lopsided, nervous grin,

"But from what I think I've heard…so are you."

Chapter 13: The Dark King

The red flames of the torches lining the black stone walls of the great hall reflected off King Mordred's dark eyes as he stared at his brother. His hand tightened repeatedly around his sword hilt, *Sceaduwe's* tip resting against the floor. Every twitch of his fingers betrayed the fury boiling beneath his skin.

When Gareth finally entered and knelt, Mordred leaned forward, hungry for good news.

"Have you found him?" he snarled.

"Not yet," Gareth replied, attempting to remain calm. "I have men searching my entire kingdom for anything unusual. We scoured the woods and found nothing. I rode after him myself–"

"THE BOY MUST BE FOUND!" Mordred roared, his voice echoing against the wall. "The lance responded to him. As it did Arthur. No commoner from South Hamtun should have been able to pull that lance from the stone!"

A dark figure stepped out of the shadows behind Mordred's throne.

"Power chooses its wielder, my king," she said in a chilling voice, "As it chose Arthur before you."

She placed a slender hand on the throne.

Gareth glanced at her, then back to Mordred, whose rage was only sharpened by her words.

"What would you have me do, my king?" Gareth asked, attempting to steady his brother. "I have already sent word to my soldiers to be on the lookout for travelers. Specifically, one carrying the weapon."

"That is a start," Mordred muttered through gritted teeth. "Tell them nothing else. We do not need to give breath to the rumors that are already spreading. I will send word to our brothers as well."

The shadowed woman approached a few steps.

"The old monk is wise," she murmured. "He will know we hunt them. They will avoid your garrison. They will avoid Eoforwic. The only safe road north is through the mountains."

At this, Mordred's fury twisted into a smirk.

"Yes. Yes, that is where they'll go. Lancelot will want to return to the monks at Dunholm, where he clearly has been hiding all these years. The coward."

He turned to Gareth.

"You will ride north. Wait to the east of the pass. If they can survive the mountains…you will be there to greet them."

"Yes, King." Gareth bowed. "And should the boy use the lance against us?"

"Then do what you must to remove it from him. Kill anyone who stands with him, especially the fool Lancelot." Mordred paused, his eyes narrowed to slits. "But bring the boy to me. Alive."

Gareth nodded once and strode from the great hall. The doors boomed shut behind him.

Mordred exhaled sharply, shaking with a fury he could barely contain. The torchlight flickered across him like blood moving beneath his skin.

The enchantress stepped forward, her voice low and precise.

"You understand what happens if the realm learns who he is."

Mordred's jaw clenched.

"They won't. I'll see him dead first."

The enchantress's eyes narrowed, studying him.

"Dead?" she echoed, softly. "Mordred...if the lance answered to him, then it has already spoken his name."

She circled him like drifting smoke.

"If the boy reaches Dunholm...if the monks shelter him...if even a whisper escapes..."

She leaned in, her voice now sharp as a razor.

"Every banner in Britain will turn from you. They will march under the hope of Arthur's son."

Mordred slammed Sceaduwe's tip into the stone, cracking the floor.

"Then he must never live long enough to be known."

A slow, chilling smile touched her lips.

"Exactly. So pray Gareth does not fail you again."

She slowly returned to the shadow.

"The mountains have teeth, Mordred." Her voice drifted like a curse.

"Gareth is merely the second bite.

Chapter 14: The Mountain

Van told them what he saw and how he ended up hiding in the barn. Earlier that morning, before the explosion, Van spotted a lone rider galloping in from the southern road. The rider looked as though he had ridden through the night. The man brought warnings to the guards as he passed, that Gareth's soldiers were hunting three travelers, one of them carrying a strange lance.

He watched as Gareth's soldiers arrived in the village. Fearing they would find him as well, he panicked…and so had his magic. A stray spark leapt from his fingertips before he could smother it, catching the grain barrels and triggering the explosion that sent the town into chaos.

"If what you heard is true, then we have less time than I thought," Lancelot said, as he analyzed the story. "We must escape and go north. If Gareth's soldiers are already here and looking for us, we can no longer travel by road. We certainly cannot pass Eoforwic, where Gareth is seated."

"They will be searching every town soon," he continued grimly. "This leaves us with only one path. We must travel through the mountains. It will be dangerous…but less dangerous than Gareth's men."

"Let me come with you." Van blurted out. "I am not welcome here any more than you are. I don't know why they are hunting you, but I do know what they'll do if they catch *me*. Magic folk are not allowed in the Kingdom without a master. I may not know how to control my magic yet, but I *can* help. Please…let me come."

Shyla, Arion, and Lancelot exchanged uncertain looks.

"I'm not sure you coming with us is any safer." Arion admitted.

Truthfully, he didn't know how much he trusted Van. The boy's magic was wild, powerful but unpredictable. He could be as much danger as help.

Lancelot nodded his head in agreement. "No. We can help you escape from Ledes, but you should go your own way. Our mission is far too dangerous. We cannot take another life into our hands."

Shyla stepped forward. "He saved our lives. He didn't mean to, but he did. And if he helped us by *accident*…imagine what he could do on purpose."

Van blinked at her, surprised. His purple eyes glowed faintly.

"Thank you," he whispered. "You know…I didn't notice it before, but you hum with the same magic as his weapon."

All three of them snapped their attention toward him.

Shyla's eyes widened. She quickly looked away.

"Well," she said briskly, "trained or untrained, anyone with magic could be useful. We have no idea what we'll face in the mountains. And at the very least, he can start a fire."

"Very well," Lancelot said, though his gaze lingered on Shyla with newfound concern. "But Van—you obey my every word. No random magic. One mistake could kill us."

Van nodded so hard his hair flopped into his eyes. "Deal."

Outside, the noise of running soldiers and screaming villagers had finally quieted. Lancelot judged it safe enough, and they slipped out, through a narrow gap in the barn wall. Snow began to fall heavily as they left Ledes behind for the looming mountains. The farther they went, the harsher the wind became.

By the time they reached the first incline, snow was falling in steady sheets.

"The snow will cover our tracks!" Lancelot shouted back.

It did. But it also turned the climb into a vicious struggle.

Lancelot pushed ahead slowly, the cold seeping deep into forgotten wounds and old joints. Shyla and Arion forged on steadily, while Van slipped and scrambled behind them...until he suddenly vanished with a yelp.

Arion looked back just in time to see Van tangled in a bush eight feet below, arms and legs sticking out like a dropped marionette.

"If I slip again," Van sputtered, "I swear I'll set this mountain on fire. By accident, of course."

Arion couldn't help but laugh as he hauled him back up.

They reached the top of the first incline and looked upon the mountain. They had been climbing for hours and had barely made it up the mountain.

With a sigh, they forged further forward through the whipping snow and wind. It was now snowing so heavily that they could barely see. Lancelot stopped at a rock face.

"There is a narrow ledge here. Watch your footing. Stay close to the mountain."

Narrow was putting it mildly. Arion took the lead and stepped on to the ledge and only the heel of his boots were on solid ground. Slowly, back against the wall, he shuffled. Shyla followed. Lancelot after her. Van was the last to follow.

They slunk along the mountain slowly, carefully placing each step. Everyone except Van, who whistled and hummed as he went, fearlessly. Shyla shook her head in disbelief.

She stumbled.

Her foot slipped as a chunk of ice broke beneath her feet.

She instinctively reached out to the closest thing to her. Arion's wrist.

Arion's heel skidded toward the edge. He grabbed *Ron* and lodged it into the mountain wall using it as a rail, the blade piercing the stone.

"Don't let go," Shyla pleaded, dangling over the cliff face.

Through gritted teeth Arion replied. "I won't. Just hold on to me."

Adrenaline took hold, and Arion pulled from both ends. Straining and using all his strength he lifted her back onto the ledge, with some help from Lancelot. Leaning against the mountain she stood for a moment trying to catch her breath and slow her heartbeat.

Arion placed his hand on her shoulder.

"You alright?"

"Yeah, I think so." Shyla shook her head, still breathing heavily.

After Shyla's nerves finally calmed, they slunk on more carefully. Until finally, they made it to proper footing on a flat shoulder of the mountain.

"You know, Arion, if you wanted to hold Shyla's hand you could have just asked her. No need to throw her off a mountain to make it happen." Van said, smiling widely.

Shyla burst out laughing. Growing red in the face as she did.

"Keep cracking jokes and you'll be the next one thrown off." Arion smiled back, happy to be on solid ground.

"Listen, heights are the least of my problems. And I'm just saying, next time you want to be romantic, choose better timing. Maybe one where we aren't about to die."

The sun was beginning to set over the horizon, as they continued their slow, cold, ascent.

"We need to climb a bit higher. Then we can look for a place to camp for the night," Lancelot shouted. He pointed to a path ahead of them, signaling for them to follow.

As they clambered on, Arion noticed markings etched in the stones nearby. He brushed the snow off of one of the stones.

"Lancelot. You need to see this."

Lancelot climbed toward him. The moment he saw the carvings, his face tightened with concern. He looked around and saw a mountain goat carcass lying torn apart nearby.

"This…is not natural," he whispered.

Attempting to hide his fear, he urged them on, his grip tightening on his swords. "Come. If we stand around any longer, we will freeze. We must continue to climb."

It was nearly pitch-black when Lancelot finally called back to them.

"The winds are growing by the minute. Let's find a place to camp."

The winds had in fact become extremely harsh. Multiple times they had to huddle together to avoid someone being knocked over, or carried back down the mountain. They found a shallow cave nearby where they were blocked from the wind and snow.

"Lancelot, can I use magic now? Just to make us a fire. Pleease?" asked Van, grinning cheesily.

"Alright. But you mustn't let it get out of control." Lancelot glanced at him, hoping he wasn't making a huge mistake

"You have my word…I think."

Van extended his hands in an attempt to conjure the fire. Nothing.

He frowned and looked at his hands.

He tried again. This time a small spark shot from his hands and hit the cold rocks, vanishing immediately.

"Aw, come on..."

Again. This time a wisp of fire emerged. It landed on the ground and smoldered, flickering for a moment.

Van looked around nervously. "It always does this. I swear."

He tried again. Pop! A firecracker sounded and a full purple flame lit up the cave.

Shyla smirked. "See, I told you he would light us a fire."

Van looked at them proudly, grinning.

They sat in silence as they drank in the fires' warmth, melting the snow and ice off their clothing.

Shyla sat with her knees pulled up, rubbing the dirt from her scraped palms. Arion kept staring at her, not worried because she may be hurt, but replaying the image of her dangling over the drop, still twisting his stomach.

Van poked the fire with a stick, sending sparks spiraling upward.

"I've always loved fire."

Shyla looked up. "Oh yea? At least this time you didn't blow anything up."

Van snorted with laughter. "I'm totally in control...mostly."

Shyla rolled her eyes, but she was smiling.

"I'll give you half credit."

Van's expression dimmed. His voice softened.

"I just want to say thank you again for saving me in Ledes. And for letting me come with you."

He looked around the room at each of their faces, lit by the purple flames.

"I know you didn't have to, but I'm glad you did. I haven't been around a group of people not chasing me or trying to kill me in a long time. I kinda forget what it feels like."

Lancelot watched him as he spoke. Not reacting, just listening.

Shyla looked at him, tears in her eyes.

"What do you mean? How long have you been alone?"

"Well, I had a master once. A real magician. Brilliant. But he was strict. So strict, I'm pretty sure he was allergic to smiling."

He grinned a little at this.

"He tried to teach me control, tried really hard. But my magic...it doesn't listen. Not the way it's supposed to."

Arion spoke up.

"So what happened?

Van stared directly into the fire as he spoke.

"He said I was too dangerous. Too unpredictable. That one day I'd get someone killed."

He looked up at Arion and Shyla, guilt shadowing his features.

"He wasn't wrong. I mean...you saw what I almost did back in Ledes. That was just one of many times where things just...happened. I've tried to learn to control it the best I could on my own. People don't trust mages without masters so I haven't stayed anywhere long. I either end up blowing something up, setting something on fire, or getting chased out of a town."

He looked back down at the fire, trying to avoid their eyes.

"You're the first people who haven't looked at me like I'm a problem since as far back as I can remember."

A single tear rolled down his cheek.

Shyla spoke softly.

"You're not a problem Van. Look. You did it here in this cave. You can control it. You just need help. We're going to find you that help. There has to be someone out there that can teach you."

Lancelot who had been silent up to this point finally spoke.

"I will not pretend I trust your magic. But I trust intent—and yours has been to help. That is enough for now."

Van wiped his cheek and looked up at Lancelot.

"Does that mean you'll keep me?

Lancelot chuckled. "If we make it off this mountain, I suppose…I will keep you." Then, with a half-grin, he followed, "But only if you promise not to set me on fire."

Van, laughing, put a hand on his heart.

"No promises."

The warmth and crackle of the fire quickly washed over them.

Arion sat looking into the fire, reflecting on all they had been through so far. The faces of those he'd lost still flickered in his mind, the pain and guilt of their loss, weighing on him harsher than the cold. He knew they had to keep going.

After a short time, they fell asleep one by one. Van found himself the last one awake. Looking around the cave, for the first time in a long time, he felt like he belonged. The thought alone was enough to make him fall asleep, smiling.

When they awoke in the morning, the wind and snow had stopped. They gathered their things and set out to finish the climb to the pass.

They stepped out of the cave with a clear view of the mountain for the first time since they began their trek. The mountain pass was visible just a short way in front of them.

As they moved nearer to the clearing of the pass, Arion began to notice more rocks with the same claw markings they found on the rocks below. Before Arion could get Lancelot's attention, Shyla called out. "Hey, there's tracks here. Some sort of animal. And they look fresh."

Lancelot took one clear look at the tracks and scanned the mountains around them. Without saying a word, he drew both swords. Following suit, Shyla nocked an arrow. Arion drew *Ron* which crackled in his grip, adrenaline beginning to spike.

"Make no sudden movements. Move with intent, but do not stop. We are not alone." Lancelot continued to scan the area on high alert.

They pushed upward until the slope opened to a flat clearing—two stone walls narrowing into a corridor beyond. The mountain pass.

"Come," Lancelot urged. "We are almost…"

BOOM!

The snow settled just long enough to reveal a silhouette. Hulking, dark, and deadly.

They were certainly not alone.

Chapter 15: The Beast

The snow flurried across the rocky clearing. A massive black hound-like creature stood growling, its ice-colored eyes shimmering through the white haze. Frosted bone-spikes jutted from its spine. Its jagged teeth dripped saliva that froze instantly on the ground.

The Barghest roared, shaking loose ice and snow that rained down upon them. They were buried by a small avalanche. Lancelot was knocked to the ground by a large mound of ice and snow.

Arion stepped out of the snowdrift, *Ron* crackling with lightning.

Van fell back screaming. "Nope, nope, nope."

Shyla loosed an arrow without hesitation.

The beast vanished in a poof of swirling snow and reappeared behind them.

"What the…" Van yelled and ran, distancing himself from the creature.

"Stay back. I've got it." Arion gripped *Ron,* and lightning swirled.

Lancelot shouted. "Arion, wait!"

But it was too late. An arc of lightning shot from the lance and exploded where the beast was standing.

A chunk of the rock platform broke and tumbled down the mountain, creating a mini avalanche of snow and stone as it rolled.

They were all thrown back from the blast, landing forcefully against the rocky wall.

The dark, icy creature stood on a ledge above them unharmed and roared again threateningly. Its eyes were fixed on *Ron*, still clutched in Arion's hand.

Slowly they each got to their feet, shaking off the impact.

"Arion!" Lancelot barked. "Lightning will collapse the mountain! You must refrain or you'll bury us all."

He turned toward the others.

"This is no ordinary hound. It is a Barghest. A beast of ice and shadow. Shyla, find a high point and fire anytime you have a clear shot. Arion, you're with me. Van, stay back!"

Shyla scrambled up the rock face. Van backed into the mouth of the pass, shaking. Arion and Lancelot rushed forward.

Shyla loosed another barrage of arrows at the beast, still barking at them from the ledge above. It again swirled into a mass of snow, and reappeared, now on the ground with Arion and Lancelot.

"A Barghest can merge with shadow, or in this case snow," Lancelot warned. "We must surprise it. Direct attacks will not work."

Shyla was like a deadly storm, raining arrows at the Barghest with chilling efficiency. Multiple more shafts jutted from the creature.

The Barghest roared with rage and turned on her. In a flash, it was on the rock face, snarling, saliva dripping, freezing as it hit the rocks.

Shyla jumped to her feet and fired a volley of arrows.

POOF!

The Barghest reappeared again, behind her. It howled, throwing saliva.

Drips of the Barghest's spit landed on the ground around Shyla, some hitting her leg. She gasped as frost crept up her leg, rooting her in place.

She tried to move. Her boots were frozen to the ground.

"Arion!! I...I can't move!"

The Barghest crouched, slinking closer to her. It reared back, ready to leap upward and finish her.

"No!!" Arion cried out in panic.

Arion reacted on instinct. He hurled *Ron* like a spear.

Lightning spiraled off the lance as it arced through the air, connecting with the Barghest mid pounce. The beast let out a shriek of pain and tumbled off the rock face.

Ron clattered in the snow next to it, bouncing when the Barghest violently landed on the platform below.

Shyla breathed out shakily, still frozen in place.

The Barghest slowly clambered to its feet, shaking off the pain as it rose.

It now turned its full attention to Arion, who was weaponless. *Ron* lay just beyond the monster's massive hind legs.

Lancelot rushed forward to help, yelling.

"Here, beast! Come and get me!"

Lancelot flashed his blades, fierceness in his eyes returning once again. He charged. His twin blades cut through empty air as the Barghest vanished, fading into snow once again.

Arion knew this was his chance. He sprinted toward his lance and slid, grabbing *Ron* in stride.

The Barghest reappeared ready to attack.

With *Ron* back in hand, Arion and Lancelot charged together.

The Barghest lunged, claws flashing like jagged ice. Arion ducked beneath one strike, sweeping *Ron* upward in a tight arc. The teal blade clipped the creature's jaw, jolting its head sideways. Lancelot then surged forward, slicing his swords across the beast's exposed flank.

For a heartbeat they fought in perfect rhythm. Lancelot's blades and Arion's lance moving like two parts of one memory, one instinct, one legacy.

Lancelot stopped for a moment, smiling gleefully, lost in battle.

The Barghest spun toward them, howling with rage.

"Arthur!...Move left!

Arion froze mid-step.

Left?

He was Arion...not Arthur...

Before he had time to respond, the Barghest's claws scraped the stone where he stood just moments before.

Lancelot snapped back to the present. He realized what he'd said. A flicker of grief and shock crossed his eyes, gone as quickly as it came.

"Forgive me. For a moment, I was back on the battlefield beside your father again."

Arion swallowed hard, stunned by the weight of the words.

But there was no time to dwell on it.

The Barghest roared and lunged again. This time right as it was about to hit the ground, it faded to snow. It reappeared directly next to Arion, and threw its head into his chest, like a battering ram. It slammed into him with its full weight.

Arion flew backward and hit the rock wall hard, head snapping against stone.

He dropped instantly, unconscious.

"Arion!!" Shyla screamed, still frozen above.

Meanwhile, Van who had finally gained the courage to join the fight scrambled up the ledge toward Shyla, slipping nervously as he climbed.

"Hang on! I got you…I think I got you…please tell me I got you."

He reached the ledge where Shyla lay, stuck to the ground. He placed his shaking hands over the ice around her legs.

"Ok. Just a little warmth. No explosions. No explosions…" He said, to try to console Shyla, and convince himself.

A tiny purple flame flickered, then sputtered out, melting a small patch of the ice.

"You're doing fine, Van." Shyla attempted convincingly. "Just…hurry"

Van glanced at her and nodded, face pale with fear.

Down below, the Barghest was rounding on Lancelot, who was growing visibly weary. Blood was running from multiple wounds, and his breath was short.

The creature roared once more and spat, shooting ice that wrapped itself around Lancelot's swords. He dropped them quickly, as the ice started creeping towards his hands. The monster lunged once again, toward the defenseless warrior.

Van watched in horror.

"No! Don't hurt him!"

Van launched a wave of fire inadvertently. The purple flames erupted, washing across the clearing. It knocked the Barghest back, while also igniting a circle of burning snow and electric-colored flame around Lancelot and the beast.

"Oh no. No, no, no…I didn't mean…I'm sorry! I didn't…" gasped Van.

The fire formed a ring, isolating Lancelot and Barghest from the others. The Barghest growled menacingly as it stared at the flames in fear.

The flames had removed the ice from Lancelot's swords, now laying in a puddle on the stone. He quickly snatched them up. Through the flame, he gave Van the faintest nod of approval, understanding the opportunity now provided. He rounded on the beast.

"If I must die so your son may live, then I gladly take that risk." Lancelot whispered softly, steadying himself. "For you, Arthur."

Lancelot whirled his swords in his hands. The Barghest growled, circling him, the ice spikes on its back steaming in the heat.

They both lunged, fire crackling around them.

Purple light reflected off the steel and icy claws as they met in midair.Both man and beast let out yelps of pain as they landed.

Then, there was silence. A mass of bone, armor, and ice lay unmoving.

Shyla, freed by the heat of the flames, ran to check on Arion. Van ran alongside her, trying to see into the flaming ring.

Arion groaned as he finally started to gain consciousness.

"What...what happened?" he said, his ears ringing.

"You nearly got yourself killed, that's what." Shyla sighed, relief washing over her.

Arion slowly got to his feet, as the flames in front of them began to die down. They could see Lancelot laying motionless beneath the Barghest.

"No! No...Lancelot!" Van yelped as they sprinted toward him.

Lancelot painfully opened one eye.

"Took you long enough." Lancelot let out a weak chuckle.

Together the three of them shoved, pushing the body of the Barghest off Lancelot. It rolled, with both of Lancelot's swords lodged firmly in its chest.

Now that he was free from the beast's body, Lancelot's own wounds became apparent. His chest was carved with three deep claw marks, bleeding heavily.

Van knelt beside him. "Please let me help. I know I messed everything up but...let me help."

Gold flickered from his palms. "I can heal him."

Arion and Shyla gave a nervous glance to each other but nodded.

Van pressed his hands to Lancelot's chest and muttered an incantation. The bleeding on the wound slowed, but barely.

"Ok. I'm not great with healing magic but that should at least keep him alive." He smiled weakly and stepped back looking exhausted.

"That...will do." Lancelot let out a weak, shaky cough. "For now. Thank you."

He looked at each of them, exhausted, proud, and wincing in pain.

Arion and Shyla gently helped him to his feet, where he stumbled for a moment.

"Thank you." Lancelot said weakly. "We must continue on. There may be more than one beast waiting for us. The way to Dunholm is just through the pass. I'll manage." He waved off Van, who was coming to put an arm around him as he walked. "Seriously, I'm okay."

Arion nodded and looked at the others. "You guys okay?"

"Yeah."

"Yep, I'm alright."

"Ok then. He's right. We're not done yet. Let's keep moving."

Arion picked up *Ron* and used it to help them stabilize Lancelot. Shyla restocked her arrows, removing some from the body of the Barghest. They began the slow walk into the narrow corridor of the pass.

Arion turned to give one last look at the smoldering corpse of the icy beast. Above them a raven circled. And somewhere beyond the snow, to the east of the mountain,

Hoofbeats echoed.

Chapter 16: The Ambush

As they came to the end of the mountain pass, the snow had slowed and the wind had died. They could see the snow-covered rolling hills just down the mountainside. They had made it through the mountain, but Lancelot was beginning to weaken even further.

"We need to get him off this mountain and get him to rest," Arion said, ushering the others forward. He was bearing most of the weight of Lancelot as they traveled. Van followed behind muttering to himself. "…stupid, reckless…I should come with warning labels…"

In just a short time, they had made it down the mountain, with relative ease considering how weak and weary they were.

"We made it," Lancelot said weakly, as they walked to the end of the rocky terrain. As they approached the base of the mountain, Arion stopped mid-stride, as a wave of unease washed him. He heard no ravens or kites, or sounds of any kind. He looked and saw a single arrow lodged in the rocks nearby. There were no individual tracks but the snow was flat ahead.

"Something's off…"

"We're nearly to Dunholm. Keep moving," urged Lancelot, exhausted.

Out of nowhere, a single arrow whipped past them, a blur of motion. On both sides, from behind the rocks, men began to emerge. They came from all angles, and quickly gathered in a shield wall around Arion and his friends. They were surrounded.

From the clearing, a massive warhorse made its way through the wall. The horse was huge, built for the cold of the North, and each breath it blew out came in heavy clouds of steam. A worn banner hung from its saddle, a black cloth with the red boar of Northumbria, stitched into it.

Arion's stomach dropped. Shyla reached for her bow. Lancelot stared for a moment before he spoke, voice tight.

"Gareth…"

Lord Gareth of Northumbria pulled his cloak back as the horse stopped in the clearing. He looked nothing like the noble knight Lancelot once knew. His armor was gleaming, edges rimmed with frost. A thick wolf-fur cloak hung over his shoulders, and snow clung to his blond hair. His face was hard—colder than the mountain wind—and his pale blue eyes held no kindness.

He looked down at them from the saddle, expression sharp and distant.

"Lancelot."

Gareth looked at Arion. "You have something that doesn't belong to you." He glanced at *Ron*, crackling in Arion's hand. "My brother, your king, wants it returned. You along with it."

He looked at Shyla and Van. "Surrender him to me and I'll spare your lives. Choose to fight and you will surely die."

"If you want me, come and get me." Arion gripped *Ron* tighter as he found the courage to face the Lord of the North. At that moment, Lancelot drew his swords and stepped forward. Despite his wounds, he planned to protect the children until his final breath.

"I thought you were dead, my old friend." Gareth snarled as he pulled a giant war axe off his back.

"And I thought you were honorable," replied Lancelot, as he stood tall once more.

Gareth smirked. "I was. Once. And then I found glory in power. In fear."

"The only thing I fear is death without honor!" Lancelot charged Gareth. At once the soldiers began to enclose. A group of Gareth's Ranger Knights hidden upon the rock wall, rained a barrage of arrows. Shyla began to nock arrows with amazing speed in return. Van, determined to prove himself, threw waves of flames holding back the shield wall in front of him.

Arion kept the wall at bay using the length of his lance. Every so often a soldier would break the ranks and he would flip *Ron* in flash and strike them down. *Ron* was crackling heavily, ready to rain lightning when called upon.

Gareth was still seated upon his horse and was locked in a fierce battle with Lancelot. Gareth charged his horse at Lancelot and swung his axe. Lancelot deflected the blow with one sword and sliced the legs of the horse with the other. Gareth went tumbling off the horse and rolled into his shield wall. His soldiers quickly helped him to his feet.

"Get off me! I don't need help. I'm going to kill that old fool!" yelled Gareth, his anger rising. Lancelot staggered as he raised his blades, preparing for more. Gareth picked up his axe and looked deadly as he marched toward Lancelot. He swung the axe down and Lancelot dodged, wincing as he did. Lancelot returned a flurry of attacks of his own, and caught Gareth in the shoulder with a blow. This only seemed to further the northern Lord's rage.

Gareth grabbed the sword with his hand and pried it from Lancelot's weakening grip. He threw it, letting it clatter against the rocks. With his hand bleeding from the blade, he gripped his axe and lunged, seemingly unaffected by the gash. Lancelot held up his lone sword to block the war axe and was knocked to the ground. Gareth landed with the whole of his weight on top of him, and the axe was driven into Lancelot's chest plate. Blood started to cover the ground, oozing from the wound.

"LANCELOT!" Arion whirled around to help him.

Gareth freed the axe from the armor and reared back, ready to deal the final blow. Arion dove and smashed into Gareth, knocking him to the ground. Gareth stood and looked at Arion deeply for the first time.

"You have your father's eyes. And his foolish sense of compassion. If you had left the old man, you three may have been able to escape while I dealt with him. Now, you will…Die!"

Gareth launched himself at Arion. Arion swiped *Ron* across the shin plates of Gareth's armor attempting to keep him at bay. The blow glanced harmless away. Gareth swung his axe and Arion dodged it with ease. The axe was impressive in size but that made it slow to swing. Every chop seemed like slow motion.

Arion could feel the calmness of battle washing over him as it did in the trials. He watched as Gareth picked up the axe once more and charged. Arion struck again with *Ron*. This time he shoved the tip of *Ron* into Gareth's shoulder where a gap in his armor showed. Gareth enraged, charged again. Arion jabbed again to the other shoulder. Gareth bellowed out this time, frustrated.

"You will not beat me! Your stolen weapon is no match for me. No matter the legend it holds! Come at me again!"

Arion could feel the power of *Ron* building as his confidence grew. He attacked in a whirl of crackling lightning, gold and teal. Gareth knelt on the ground with multiple new punctures to his armor. He breathed heavily each breath harder than the last. Arion steadied himself to end the battle when he heard screams of pain behind him.

Van had been struck with an arrow and his flame wall was beginning to fade. Van staggered, the arrow buried deep in his shoulder. He looked exhausted as he held up his single good arm, attempting to keep the flames alive.

"Arion!" he said, grunting in pain. "I don't know how much longer I can hold them!"

Shyla stood beside him, bloody and visibly weary, still shooting a barrage of arrows at the ranks of soldiers.

She aimed an arrow at the final Ranger Knight hiding in the rocks above them. The arrow struck, felling her foe. But the shield wall advanced. The soldiers were breaking the formation and beginning to charge.

"Arion!" she gasped. She grabbed for an arrow, realizing her stock was running low.

Arion looked around him.

Gareth was getting to his feet again. Smiling devilishly, as he saw their luck was about to run dry. Any moment Van and Shyla would be overrun. Lancelot still lay unmoving on the ground, barely breathing.

Arion began to feel helpless. He couldn't beat Gareth. He couldn't save his friends. All they had worked for was about to be over. Whatever his destiny was supposed to be, had failed. He was about to die. His friends were about to die. This was the end.

He was no heir to the throne. He was no son of Arthur. Just a common boy from South Hamtun.

South Hamtun—

The image of his mother flashed in his mind. Then, the image of Arthur. The Pendant. Camelot. It suddenly all made sense.

"No...I am the heir of the Pendragon." He heard himself say out loud. Breathing deeply, the world around him seemed to stop as he grabbed *Ron* with a new vigor.

"I...AM THE HEIR OF THE PENDRAGON!" he yelled.

All at once, thunder struck above him. Golden light crackled all around him, enshrouding him. The energy continued to build up within him, pressing on him, until he could not bear it any longer.

He slammed *Ron* into the ground. A shockwave rippled through the ground and radiated around him. The sound was like the world cracking open. Energy pulsed, surging outward.

Gareth and his men were knocked violently to the ground. The rocky mountain around them began to shake, crumbling. Rocks began to fall all around them, rolling off the mountain. Gareth's men ran in fear of being crushed, terrified of the power they were witnessing.

Shyla and Van were covered by the same energy that surrounded Arion. The golden light encased them all. The world quaked around them, until finally the shockwave calmed and the world stopped shaking. Arion leaned against Ron exhausted.

"Now that was some power!" Van exclaimed as he ran to Arion's side.

Arion had barely gotten to his feet when he heard the crunch of snow behind him. Somehow, Gareth had survived the shockwave.

His armor hung in pieces. His face was bloodied. One shoulder sagged unnaturally, but the rage in his eyes hadn't dimmed at all. He dragged his axe behind him, leaving a long trail in the snow.

"You…" Gareth growled, voice shaking with fury and disbelief. "You are nothing. You hear me? NOTHING. A child with a stolen name!" He raised the axe with both trembling hands. "And I will rip it from you!"

Arion tried to lift *Ron,* but exhaustion ran through him like ice. His arms felt like stone. Gareth roared and charged. Arion braced for the blow.

A sharp *thwip* cut through the air—then a hollow thud.

Gareth stopped mid-stride. He looked down. An arrow jutted cleanly from the center of his chest plate, buried so deep only the fletching remained visible. For a moment he stared at it in confusion, swaying on his feet. Slowly, he turned his head toward the ridge. Shyla stood there, bow still drawn, blood on her cheek, eyes blazing.

"You're wrong," she said, voice steady, "he's everything this kingdom needs."

Gareth's axe slipped from his fingers. He collapsed to his knees, breath catching in his throat. His eyes flicked back to Arion—not with hatred now, but something closer to fear.

"You…really are…his son," he rasped.

Then he fell face-first into the snow, unmoving.

The clearing was now filled with silence. A lone raven flew overhead. Arion exhaled shakily. Van stood frozen, wide-eyed. Shyla lowered her bow, her hands trembling for the first time. At Gareth's side, something gleamed in the snow. A small stone pendant, shaped like a teardrop and etched with strange runes. Shyla picked it up and placed it in her pocket. Arion limped back to Lancelot and dropped to his knees beside him.

"Hold on," he whispered. "We're almost to Dunholm."

The four of them didn't stay long on the battlefield. Lancelot was fading fast, and Arion and Shyla had to take turns keeping him on his feet. Van did his best to help, though he muttered anxiously the entire climb down the last ridge.

They traveled in silence, too shaken and exhausted to speak. The snow covered their tracks behind them, burying Gareth's body and the shattered ground where Arion had stood. Only once they saw the distant torchlights along the ridge did Lancelot find the strength to speak.

"Dunholm," he whispered.

They moved toward it, half-carrying their wounded mentor, not stopping until the gates opened and the monks ran to meet them.

They had made it.

Chapter 17: The Stone

The monks of Dunholm rushed out to meet the weary and battered group. Lancelot barely made it three steps past the gate before his legs gave out; the others caught him and carried him inside. They were led into the infirmary, where monks quickly ran to check on each of them. They were each shone to a bed. Arion watched as the monks laid Lancelot onto a bed and began to remove his armor.

Van, the arrow still stuck in his shoulder, lay down on the bed next to him. Shyla stood next to Van as the monks began to work, dislodging the arrow. She was exhausted, but refused their aid.

Arion was helped into his bed and a monk tried removing his armor.

"I'm fine. Just worn out. Tend to the others first." Arion waved off the monk politely. The monk bowed and turned to help with Lancelot.

Arion took a deep breath and tension washed from his body as he relaxed for the first time in days. Shyla walked over to him and touched his cheek, then grabbed his hand and smiled. The world around him slipped into darkness, Shyla's smile burning in his mind, as he fell asleep.

When he awoke the next morning, Lancelot lay bandaged in the bed across from him, still fast asleep, but alive. Van was also still asleep in his bed. Shyla was already awake, watching each of them from her bed.

"How are you feeling?" she said as she put her hand on his arm, springing from her cot.

"I'm good now. Definitely feeling sore," Arion replied as he sat up.

"Good," Shyla said beaming. "You had us all worried. Had me worried."

"So what exactly happened to you at the mountain pass? You exploded with energy. You were crackling with lightning and then boom! The ground shook, everything was blown back. It was amazing."

Arion smiled at her. "Honestly I have no idea. I just knew that if I didn't do something we were all going to die. I couldn't let that happen. And then I just felt the energy come over me. After that, I sort of blacked out."

"Well whatever it was, if you hadn't done it, we wouldn't be here." Shyla gazed at Arion proudly. "So thank you." She rubbed his arm gently.

Arion went suddenly red. "Well, really I should be thanking you. If you hadn't taken that shot and put Gareth down, *I* might not be here." He gingerly got to his feet. He grabbed Shyla and pulled her in close, wrapping his arms around her. "Thank you. And thank you for believing in me."

"Is this a group hug situation?" Van was awake and grinning from ear to ear. "Because if so, be gentle with me. I got shot with an arrow, remember."

Arion and Shyla separated, stepping apart quickly, both red with embarrassment.

Just as he sat up, Lancelot let out a groan.

Van leapt from his bed, and stood beside Lancelot. They all stood around him as he opened his eyes. He glanced at each of them as they looked upon him with concern.

"It will take more than Gareth and an overgrown dog to take me down." Lancelot joked feebly.

They all gave a sigh of relief, laughing gently.

"Though...I confess, much of the fight is smoke in my mind. I remember precious little after the beast. Remind me how we ended up here."

They sat and relived the tales of the battle. How Van and Shyla held the army at bay with magic and arrows. How Arion had defeated the army and Gareth with his explosive power. And how Shyla had ultimately put Gareth down for good.

"I thank all of you for the honor and valiant courage you showed to get us here safely. I am sorry I could not do more," he whispered shamefully for a moment, but then smiled brightly. "I am proud of each of you. Yes, even you, Van." Van laughed but beamed with pride. "Arion, I cannot explain what happened to you either. I have never seen magic like what you describe. This must be another secret of the Pendragon that even your father was never able to tap into. You are special in so many ways. Arthur would be proud of you."

Arion tried to fight back the tears that were welling in his eyes. "Thank you, sir."

Lancelot slowly sat himself up further, wincing and groaning as he did so.

"While we are safe here in these walls, King Mordred will not stop until Arion has been found, captured or killed. Any soldier who survived the battle will have begun to tell the tales of what they witnessed. Mordred will be infuriated by this news. The tales will give more legitimacy to any rumors that may have been swirling already about you, Arion, and who you are. We will stay here and prepare. The battle may have been won, but I believe the war is just beginning."

All three of them nodded in agreement. They had come so far in a short time but they knew their journey was far from over.

"Arion, I will personally train you, once I am healed. Van, the monks here are versed in some magic and I would like you to train with them, to at least learn to control your magic. Shyla, there is an archery range in the concourse I think you will find to your liking. We will stay until we have gathered our strength. We will not wait for Mordred to come knocking on our door. A sign will come to lead us to our next destination." Lancelot said with a renewed determination.

"Actually, I think I may have something." Shyla pulled the stone out of her pocket and showed them all the rune markings on the teardrop-shaped rock. "This fell off Gareth's armor when he hit the ground. I had seen runes before but this one looked different. I thought it was too important to leave on the ground."

Lancelot looked at the rune with intense focus and reached out his hand. Shyla handed him the rune.

"This is one of Merlin's runes. You said this fell off his armor?" Shyla nodded. "This could very well explain the rage that Gareth showed during the battle. During my time with Gareth, I had never seen an anger like that in him. This rune would have given him incredible strength, along with the rage. I do not know how he could have come upon it. No one has heard from Merlin since the fall of Arthur."

Van's eyes grew wide as he stared at the rune.

"Merlin! No way! May I see it?" Van asked, reaching out his hand.

Lancelot handed him the rune, with great concern on his face. As soon as the rune was in Van's grasp, he began to grow white. His purple eyes were now colorless. His body became still...

An old man with overgrown white wispy hair and a long white beard lay on a rocky floor. He looked malnourished and feeble. A long chain clasped around his ankle bound him to the wall. There's a sound of a cell door opening. A shadow of a dark hooded figure loomed over him and dropped old bread and a nearly rotten apple on the ground next to him. The old man lifted his head slightly off the ground and whispered between each breath. "Find me.. heir of...Pendragon...Help me...before...too late."

Arion was standing over Van trying to shake him, yelling his name.

"Van! Van! Are you okay!? Van! Wake up! Wake Up!"

Van jerked back to consciousness. Purple returned to his eyes. He was drenched in sweat, heart racing. He stood up quickly, fumbling for words.

"You're...you're not going to believe what I just saw."

He explained to them the vision he just had. The old man. The message. He didn't know how he knew...but he was certain: he had just seen Merlin.

Lancelot sat up fully at hearing this.

"If Merlin lives, this changes everything. There is greater hope still."

He stood and placed his hand on Arion's shoulder.

"If Merlin calls for you, then we must find him. The Kingdom of Camelot hangs in the balance. And only you can save it... Arion Pendragon.

Epilogue: The Ascension

Weeks had passed since they arrived at Dunholm, battered and bruised. Snow was beginning to melt. The winds were warming. Arion and Lancelot had started their training sessions in the open courtyard. Sunlight flickered off *Ron* as Arion swung it, arcing and gleaming. Lancelot, still bandaged from the battles in the mountains, used a training pole to demonstrate movements and defensive tactics for Arion to mimic.

Lancelot spun his stick, creating a whirling shield as it twirled between both hands. Arion copied the movement, then added a slash at the end, which knocked Lancelot back, and he fell to the ground..

Lancelot groaned in pain as he landed.

"I'm sorry! Are you alright?" Arion hurried to Lancelot's side to help.

"Yes, yes. I'm okay. I've recovered from worse." Lancelot chuckled as he was helped to his feet.

He looked at Arion proudly.

"You really are a natural. Even your father didn't progress as quickly as this."

"Well, if you trained him this hard, I can see why he was such a feared warrior." Arion wiped the sweat from his face.

"Hard?" Lancelot grinned slyly. "We're just getting started." He playfully struck Arion in the back with his training pole.

They laughed as they continued the training session.

Nearby, in the concourse, Shyla crouched on a narrow ledge, bow pulled taut. She fired an arrow at a small target, striking it with perfect accuracy. She then leapt from her roost and grabbed a rope, lowering herself slowly. She wrapped the rope around one leg, hanging upside down as she loosed another arrow at the target. Perfect strike again.

She flipped herself and unraveled from the rope, spinning. She landed on the ground in a heroic crouch, knees bent, bow behind. She then sprung from the position and sprinted toward a climbing wall. Instead of climbing she kicked off the wall, flipping herself feet-over-head. Mid-flip, she fired another arrow at the target. This time, her arrow landed with such precision, it split her previous arrow in half.

She landed to a small round applause from nearby monks, and Arion, who was watching captivated by her every move, as he entered the concourse.

"You make that look easy."

Shyla smirked, as she dusted off her knees. "You watch all your friends like that, or just the pretty ones?"

Her face became more serious. "My father used to say that skill is the one thing no one can take from you. Not fear, not kings...not even death."

Arion stepped closer. "You miss him."

She nodded, swallowing. "Every day. But when I shoot my bow...it feels like he's still guiding my hands." She looked up at Arion, voice lowering. "And when I look at you...I feel like everything he hoped for might actually be possible."

She pulled him in close and they embraced in a hug. They held each other for a moment longer before Shyla pulled back, brushing a loose strand of hair behind her ear.

"Come on," she said softly. "We should check on Van. He's been working with the monks a lot lately on controlling his magic...something about wanting to "master the fire before it masters him."

Arion laughed, shaking his head.

"Right, before he burns Dunholm down."

They walked together toward the inner halls. Van knelt alongside three monks in a candlelit chamber. They were working on breathing slowly and controlled. Purple flames flickered between his palms.

First, it was just a small spark, growing to a medium fireball. It was suddenly a small spark again.

"Fire listens to the calm hand," one monk said calmly, encouraging Van. "Not the angry one. You cannot control fire with fire."

Without warning, a flaming plume erupted from his hands, singeing his eyebrows. All three monks sighed in unison.

Van looked up and saw Shyla and Arion waiting for him. He smiled proudly.

"Hey, that's an improvement! Last time I burned down a chicken coop."

They all laughed deeply as they left the chamber, their voices echoing down the stone hall.

But as they disappeared around the corner, Van's smile slowly faded. He stopped for a moment, letting the others slip ahead.

He watched as the monks began extinguishing candles one by one. Shadows stretched along the walls.

He stood there...alone again, like so many nights before. Then he reached into his pouch, and pulled out the rune, flipping it over in his hands.

He could feel it hum softly…insistently.

Van swallowed.

"Come on," he whispered. "I know there's got to be more. Show me more."

He gripped the rune and closed his hands. Purple flames flickered playfully around his hands. Controlled this time. The stone glowed faintly in response.

Van's eyes flipped white. Body rigid once more.

Merlin was still chained to the wall, breathing weakly on the rocky floor. A torch flickered behind him. The image of a great stag was crested on the wall. Roots could be seen breaking through the stone above. A small trickle of water formed a pool where the chain connected to the sandy-colored wall.

Van returned to the dark room, shaking.

He rushed to find Lancelot, Shyla, and Arion. He reached them in the meal hall, out of breath, sweating and scrambling to find his words.

"It worked! The rune worked."

He showed them the rune, still faintly glowing in his hand. "I saw Merlin again."

He looked at them, purple eyes blazing with excitement.

"I know where he is."

COMING SOON

BOOK TWO IS COMING.
ARION PENDRAGON SURVIVED THE
MOUNTAIN… BUT SURVIVAL HAS A COST.

MORDRED STILL RULES.

THE BROTHERS OF LOT STILL HUNT.

AND THE TRUTH OF ARTHUR'S HEIR CANNOT
REMAIN HIDDEN FOR LONG.

AS THE KINGDOM BEGINS TO STIR, OLD
MAGIC AWAKENS, ALLIANCES ARE TESTED,
AND ENEMIES RISE THAT CANNOT BE OUT-
RUN.

THE WAR FOR BRITAIN HAS NOT BEGUN YET.
BUT IT IS COMING.

*PENDRAGON RISING: BOOK TWO — COMING
SOON.*

www.ingramcontent.com/pod-product-compliance
Lightning Source LLC
Chambersburg PA
CBHW071129100726
47908CB00008B/2549